D0800587

THE CHRISTMAS
KEY

Other books by Kim O'Brien:

Legal Weapon

THE CHRISTMAS KEY

•

Kim O'Brien

Montlake Romance

Text copyright ©2005 by Kim O'Brien
All rights reserved.
Printed in the United States of America.

na # 6 2 5 /
(6 3 5 4)

Published by Montlake Romance
P.O. Box 400818
Las Vegas, NV 89140

ISBN-13: 9781477813997
ISBN-10: 1477813993

This title was previously published by Avalon Books; this version has been reproduced from the Avalon book archive files.

For almost getting us locked in a church, I dedicate this book with love to my amazing husband, Michael. I also could not have written this book without the love and support of my daughters, Beth and Maggie, who daily make me realize how blessed I am. I also thank my mother, Laurie Sutton, who spoils all of us (but we love and appreciate it!). Above all, the credit goes to the good Lord who makes all things possible.

Chapter One

7:45 p.m.—Joanie

"Dear Friends and Family,

"Well, it's certainly been a memorable year."

Pen in hand, Joanie Williams paused. *Think cheerful*, she ordered herself. *Tomorrow is Christmas Eve and this is supposed to be a happy letter.*

She chewed the end of her pen and mulled over the year. Something good had to have happened, but for the life of her, she couldn't think of a single thing. A stack of cards sat at her elbow. All of them contained news of happy families, great vacations, and high-achieving children.

Frowning, she stared at the Christmas stationery. For the past two weeks she'd been trying to come up with something positive, and always the page remained stubbornly blank. Now she was running out of time. If she didn't write something now, she'd never get the cards postmarked before Christmas.

Sighing, Joanie imagined what her friends would think if she simply told them the truth about her year. Putting the pen to paper, she slowly began to write.

"Natalie is flunking three subjects, so she won't be graduating from high school this June. Amy has pierced her body in so many places we've lost count. Boris, our basset hound, has developed irritable bowel syndrome, which is not as bad as it seems as we need to replace the carpet anyway because of the leak in the fish tank.

"But the crown jewel is my divorce, which came through in June. Mitchell and I haven't spoken directly to each other in months, which my support group at church says . . ."

Uh oh. Her Suddenly Single support group was meeting tonight. Joanie checked her watch. It was 7:45 p.m. She groaned. The meeting started in fifteen minutes.

Joanie quickly grabbed her car keys. As she sprinted for the door, she noticed Boris standing by the back door. When he saw her looking at him, he wagged his tail. A thin line of drool seemed to underscore the tragic look in his enormous brown eyes. Why did he have to pick now to go out? She'd be even later if she waited for him to do his business. Yet she couldn't just leave him.

"You'll have to hurry." Joanie put her hand on the knob. Boris leaned hard against the wooden door, preventing her from opening it.

"Back up," she urged the dog, who had begun panting at an alarming rate and leaned even harder against the door.

"Oh for goodness sakes." Joanie bent in frustration, put her arms around the dog's chest, and gently pushed him backward. As the dog's smooth pads slid on the polished wood floors, Joanie heard the unmistakable hissing sound, like air being released from a balloon.

Great. This is just great, she thought, as Boris disappeared out the door. *I'm not only going to be late, but also I'm going to show up smelling like a dog fart.* Why hadn't these things ever happened to Mitchell?

Joanie was still thinking about this as she got into her old Jeep Cherokee. She wished she were more like her ex-husband, who had an undeniable talent for being far from the scene whenever things got tough. She could almost hear his voice whispering that the dog was the kids' responsibility and she wouldn't be late to her meeting if she made the girls take care of Boris.

Well, Joanie decided, she probably didn't smell that bad. She might be a few minutes late, but she was doing the best she could. At least she was trying, and not pointing out everybody else's failings, or hiding behind that lame excuse about having to work late, as Mitchell usually did. *Owning a music store is not a nine-to-five job, blah, blah, blah.*

Okay, enough already, she ordered herself. *Stop hearing Mitch's voice in your head. You're divorced, right? This is what you wanted. You're happier.*

But was she? Joanie found her thoughts shying away from the question that had haunted her ever since her divorce became final in October. Had ending her marriage been the right thing? Here it was, six months since their divorce, and she was more miserable than ever.

Joanie pressed the gas pedal a little harder. She and Mitch had been married for nearly twenty years, and if they couldn't work out their problems in that space of time, they never would.

Around her, the night soaked the earth in darkness. The December freeze penetrated the car despite the heater going full blast. Above, stars dotted the sky. Joanie thought how the stars on this night so long ago had guided the Wise Men to the baby Jesus. She longed for the stars to guide her as well. However, lately when she looked up at them, all she saw were millions of tiny dots lost in the pattern of a world that seemed more confusing every day.

She turned onto the long, curving driveway of Faith Community Church. Under the streetlights, the gnarled limbs of oaks shuddered under a gust of wind. *Here comes that rainstorm the weatherman promised*, Joanie thought, belatedly remembering she'd left her umbrella at home.

In the distance, an outdoor nativity scene glittered with tiny white Christmas lights. Something about the sight of Mary and Joseph bending over the rough cradle and the angels pointing their trumpets heavenward made Joanie's throat tighten.

Pulling into a parking space, Joanie turned off the engine and gathered her wool coat tightly around her. Perversely, she couldn't make herself get out of the car although each moment made her later and later.

She looked at the old stone building in the distance, automatically studying the juniper bushes, the silver leaves of the caladium and holly vines spilling from containers near the doors. Even to a professional eye, she could find no fault with the landscaping. The plants were as healthy and well-tended as the ones in the nursery she managed.

Come on, Joanie, she ordered herself. *You can do this. Just get out of the car.*

Swinging the door open, she stepped into the night, made even colder by a wind that seemed to blow straight through her wool coat. Joanie put her hand on her head as her hair whipped around her face. With determination, she headed toward the church.

Lights inside the building burned brightly, a promise of the warmth and friendship waiting inside. Walking more quickly now, Joanie arranged her expression into something upbeat and cheerful. As she neared the entrance, she spotted several dead blooms in the patch of winter pansies.

Despite the cold, Joanie found herself unable to resist bending and pinching off a handful of dead heads and let the wind carry them off.

Straightening, she surveyed her work. *Better*, she thought. *Funny what a little soil can do for a girl's spirits.*

She wiped her fingers on a tissue and then pulled open the church's heavy oak door.

Chapter Two

8:10 p.m.—Joanie

Just as Joanie stepped inside, the wind picked up again. It practically pushed her inside and slammed the door behind her with such a mighty bang that she cringed in embarrassment.

She entered the chapel, expecting someone to tease her about projecting her anger onto the church door. However, glancing around, she saw row after row of empty pews.

Joanie walked deeper inside the church. Had she gotten the time wrong? Spotlights from high-above beams illuminated an empty room. What in the world was going on?

"Hello," Joanie called. "Anyone here?"

7

Her voice echoed in the clear acoustics of the church. "Hello," Joanie called again, wondering if this were some kind of joke and in a minute everyone would jump out and yell "surprise."

"Joanie?"

Spinning around, Joanie stared in amazement. "Mitch, what in the world are *you* doing here?"

"What do you mean what am I doing here?" Mitch replied. "What are *you* doing here?"

Joanie pulled her coat more tightly around herself and tried to recover from the sight of her ex-husband in the church. "I have a meeting," she stated. "My group gets together every Wednesday night at 8:00."

"It's the night before Christmas Eve," Mitch pointed out. "Don't you think that most groups would have cancelled their meetings?"

"*You're* here," Joanie stated and lifted her eyebrows.

"That's different," Mitch replied. "My meeting is with Pastor Frank, and he set it up himself."

"Why would he do that?" Joanie asked. "When he knows that the Suddenly Singles group has the downstairs meeting room reserved?"

Mitch shrugged. "If your group is supposed to meet here, where are they?"

Joanie swallowed. From the expression on his face, she knew he thought she'd been the one to get the time wrong. She shifted her weight. Had she been watering the poinsettias when the meeting had been changed?

"If you were supposed to meet Pastor Frank," she said at last, "where is he?"

"Probably late," Mitch said.

"Well, my group probably is already downstairs."

"Nope," Mitch informed her. "I just came from there. It's empty."

Empty? Joanie swallowed. This never had happened before. And if it had to happen now, why did it have to be on the very evening her ex-husband happened to be there?

"I'll just go see," Joanie said, mainly to get away from him and give herself a chance to think.

A quick check of the lower level only proved Mitch correct. Returning to the chapel, she found Mitchell sitting in the same pew. He had his head bent, displaying the gap between his hair and the collar of his overcoat. She noticed his hairline, ragged and uneven. In the past, she had kept this neat and even for him.

"You're right," she admitted. "We're alone."

Mitchell shrugged. "Pastor Frank hasn't shown up yet either."

Joanie checked her watch. "Maybe everyone's running late."

"We could give them another five minutes," Mitch agreed.

As they sat in silence, Joanie looked around the

chapel. It was an old church, lovingly restored. The wood panels gleamed in a dark, rich stain, which contrasted with the plain white trim on the window panels. Garlands of evergreens looped through the aisles; white candles lined the windows. At least fifty poinsettia plants bloomed on the steps to the altar. If she hadn't been so heart-heavy, she would have thought the old church breathtakingly beautiful.

"So how have you been, Joanie?"

Lousy. "Fine." She studied the scuff mark on her favorite pair of black boots. "You?"

"Busy," Mitch said. "The shop's doing really well this season. Drum sets are big."

"That's nice." Joanie toyed with a button on her coat. Only too well she remembered Amy's early efforts. Now, of course, it was a much more rhythmic thumping, with longer, more complex drum rolls, but it still made the kitchen floor vibrate.

"You got my child support check, right?"

"Yes, Mitch." One thing about Mitch, he made sure he provided financially for the girls. "Thank you," she added, sounding a bit stiff but unable to be otherwise.

"You're welcome," Mitch replied. "And thank you for switching weekends with me next month."

"You're welcome," Joanie said, thinking they sounded exactly like a divorced couple reduced to politeness because there was nothing else left between them.

"Natalie told me that you've been working some long hours yourself at the Garden Center."

What else had Natalie told him about her? Joanie felt her chest tighten. She hoped her eldest daughter hadn't talked about the personal stuff—the weight she'd gained because she needed to fill up the empty places inside, or the nights she sat up watching television because sleep eluded her. Or, heaven forbid, the time she'd been caught looking through old photo albums and crying.

"It's the holiday season," Joanie said lamely. "What can I say? Everyone wants a poinsettia."

Mitch pointed to the rows of the red-leafed plant. "Those from your nursery?"

Joanie nodded. "Yeah. Want one? We've still got a couple hundred in our greenhouse."

"You know me and plants," Mitch said. "I kill the artificial ones."

This wasn't true, at least Joanie didn't think so. But then, when they'd been married, he'd never had to water a single plant. She had always been there to do it for him.

Restless, she walked to the front of the church where the double rows of poinsettia plants lined the steps leading to the stage area.

Kneeling, Joanie tried to console herself with the

spongy feeling of the soil on her fingers. *It's a little dry*, she thought. *These poor babies could use a drink.*

She was about to head for the kitchen area for water when Mitch's voice just behind her made her jump.

"I think I'll run by Pastor Frank's office in the administration building." Mitchell pushed his coat sleeve back to check his watch. "If he isn't here by now, he's never coming."

Joanie couldn't remember seeing a light in that building when she'd driven past, but didn't say anything. Mitchell would just disagree—the way he always did.

Since she didn't want to be in the church alone, Joanie decided to leave with him. She'd come back in the morning, when Pastor Frank was there, to water the plants.

Following Mitchell to the front door of the church, she watched him twist the brass knob. Nothing happened.

Turning, he frowned at her and tried again. When the door didn't budge the third time, he gripped it harder and leaned against the door. When it remained shut, he took a step backward and threw his shoulder against the thick, varnished wood.

"Mitchell!" Joanie cried. "What are you doing?"

Mitchell rubbed his shoulder. "The darn door's stuck." He narrowed his gaze at it.

Joanie tried the door. "It's not stuck," she said, "it's locked."

Mitchell's eyebrows rose. "What do you mean, it's locked?"

"Locked," Joanie repeated slowly, "as in you need a key to get it open."

Shaking his head, Mitchell studied the door. "I can't believe it." He turned to her. "You must have locked it when you came in."

The hair on the back of Joanie's neck prickled. Why did he always have to blame her for everything? She narrowed her gaze. "What do you mean *I* must have locked it?"

"You were the last person inside."

Joanie's jaw tightened. "I didn't lock it."

"I heard the way you slammed it when you got here," Mitch said. "You probably tripped the lock."

"I didn't slam it," Joanie stated. "The wind caught it."

"Was there a key in the lock when you came in?"

"I don't think so." In truth, she had been hurrying and hadn't paid much attention.

"Maybe something fell out on the other side." Mitch lay down on the slate floor and tried to look underneath the door. After a moment he straightened and pushed his dark blond hair off his forehead. "I don't see anything."

Joanie tried the door one final time. She couldn't budge it an inch. "What if we're locked inside here?"

For a moment their gazes locked. Joanie saw that the idea of being stuck in the church with her was just as horrifying to him as it was to her.

"We can't be locked in," Mitch said, already in motion.

"Where are you going?"

He didn't pause, but called over his shoulder. "We're going to find a way out of here, that's what."

Chapter Three

The front door proved to be the only exit from the first level, so Joanie led the way to the basement. Round tables furnished a huge room simply decorated with industrial gray carpeting and cream-colored walls. Framed crayon drawings, drawn by children, illustrated commands to *Love One Another, Forgive One Another*, and *Serve One Another*.

Walking past the artwork, Joanie couldn't help but think that she and Mitch had failed every one of these simple instructions. How had everything become so complicated between them? Even five-year-olds seemed to have their priorities more clearly defined than they had had.

Striding across the room, Mitch pointed triumphantly to a set of walk-out doors. "I knew it," he said.

The smile disappeared from his lips when these doors proved to be as stubbornly locked as the one on the main floor. Silently he prowled the windowless room.

His frown deepened as he walked into the basement kitchen. Following closely behind, Joanie fought the feeling of despair. She'd been in that kitchen before and knew there wasn't an exit there either.

Putting her hands on her hips, she surveyed the gleaming white countertops and polished stainless steel sink. The kitchen looked nothing like her own, which daily seemed to breed clutter.

"I can't believe it," Mitch said. "You mean to tell me there are only two doors in this whole building? Just how did it ever manage to pass a fire safety inspection?"

Reminding herself she wasn't responsible for the church's ability to meet safety codes, Joanie nonetheless felt compelled to explain. "It has a state-of-the-art sprinkler system."

"There's got to be a spare key somewhere in here." Mitch began opening and closing drawers. Joanie tried not to wince at the angry sound of them banging closed. He must really want to get out of the church and away from her.

Joanie opened an upper cabinet. "This one's empty."

"So's this one." Mitch banged another drawer closed. "I can't believe I left my cell phone in the car."

That makes two of us, Joanie thought, remembering how she used to accuse him of having it permanently attached to his ear.

"Do you have your cell phone?" Mitch asked.

Joanie smiled smugly. She should have thought of that from the beginning. "Of course."

But when she reached into her purse, she couldn't find it. "I must have left it at home."

Mitchell sighed. She knew he was dying to give her a hard time, but since he was just as much at fault as she, he couldn't. After a moment he pointed up at a set of high, narrow windows above the kitchen countertops. "We're going out through those."

Gazing at the metal, black panes holding the glass in place, Joanie decided they looked more like decorative windows than functional ones. "Mitchell . . ." she began.

He glared down at her. "What?"

That look in his eyes was still there. The look that said he blamed her for being stuck in the church and for everything bad that happened between them.

She swallowed. She hated when he looked at her

as if she were a flat tire on his car. Something inside her sank. She closed her mouth. "Nothing."

Climbing onto the countertop, Mitchell knelt on the Formica surface. Grasping the sill with both hands, he took a deep breath and began to lift.

As the seconds passed by, Joanie watched the color in her ex-husband's face go from tan to red, then to dark red and then to eggplant purple. She touched his leg. "Mitch? You okay?"

Breathing hard, Mitchell released the window. "I'm fine," he said. "The window is stuck."

Of course the window was stuck. She could have told him that if he hadn't given her such an accusing look. Still, Joanie couldn't help feeling slightly responsible for getting them locked in the church. "I'll help you."

Pointedly avoiding the hand he extended, she scrambled up on the counter. She didn't want him to touch her, or even have him so close to her.

"Grab the sill, here," Mitchell directed. "When I count to three, we both push up."

Light glinted off the thick band of Mitchell's wedding ring. Joanie stared at it, amazed he still wore it. Her own sat at the bottom of her jewelry box wrapped in tissue paper so she would not have to look at it.

"Joanie?"

Startled, she hoped he wouldn't comment on the way she had looked at his ring. Instead, she stared out the window into the blackness and the even darker shapes of tall pines. His skin smelled clean like those pines. She wished he would not press his shoulder so near.

"One . . . two . . . three."

Joanie lifted with all her might. "It's stuck," she gasped.

"Push harder," Mitchell ordered.

"I *am*," Joanie grunted.

"Keep going."

"I'm pushing so hard I'm seeing spots."

"Okay," Mitchell gasped. "Let go."

In relief Joanie released the windowsill. Blinking, she watched a few more white dots float past her vision. "You don't think I'm having a brain hemorrhage, do you?"

This would be the final straw, to faint dead away on the kitchen floor of the church. Mitchell would probably stand over her, demanding that she get up and not seeing that she was dying before his eyes. This was the trouble in their marriage, she thought. He had only seen what he wanted to see.

"You're not having a brain hemorrhage," Mitchell stated. "This time, when I push, you bang something against the side of the window."

Joanie carefully climbed off the countertop and looked for something to hit against the window. A quick search yielded an aluminum frying pan. It was slightly larger than she liked, but other than a huge pasta pot there wasn't anything else.

Climbing back into position next to Mitchell, she showed him the fry pan. "I'm ready."

He frowned at the pan. "We want to get out of here—not make an omelet."

"Very funny." Joanie raised the pan. "Lift the darn window and let's get out of here."

"You're going to hit the window, right?"

"No, I'm going to hit you on the head." Joanie released her breath impatiently. "Now lift."

Mitchell took a deep breath and strained to raise the window. At the same time, Joanie fixed her gaze on a spot on the side of center of the sill. The glint of Mitchell's wedding ring caught her eye again. *It's like a magnet. I have to stop looking at it.*

"Joanie," Mitchell gasped. "Just do it."

He's a musician. He'll kill me if I hit his hands. She swung the pan. It arced through the air, missed Mitchell's nose by centimeters, and smashed into the window. One of the glass panes shattered upon impact, but the window remained stubbornly closed. For a moment neither of them spoke as cold air flowed through the jagged hole.

Mitchell's face looked pale. "Thank God that wasn't my head."

Joanie swallowed. "You try if you think you can do it so much better."

Mitch shook his head. "Mark McGwire should have your swing."

"Who's Mark McGwire?"

"A very famous baseball player."

"Stop making fun of me," Joanie ordered. "And start thinking about what we should do next to get out of here."

"Maybe you could try whacking the front door with the fry pan. I'll bet you ten dollars the hinges go by the third hit."

"Get real. I'm not hitting anything else with this." Joanie put the skillet down carefully on the counter. "I think we should go back to the chapel and wait for someone to come."

"You're giving up already?"

"The window is sealed shut, Mitch. I could whack it all day and we wouldn't get anywhere."

Mitch snorted. "What about trying something else? We could work together to find another way out."

Joanie laughed without humor. "Work together? We can't even be in the same room together."

"We could if you'd try," Mitch replied. "If you ask me, you give up way too easily."

"I didn't ask you," Joanie retorted, afraid Mitch might be talking about more than the window.

"That's right," Mitch shot back. "You don't ask. You just do."

Another reference to their failed marriage. Joanie

bit her lip. She knew exactly where it was leading and had no desire to revisit the reasons she'd initiated their divorce. Those poinsettias upstairs needed water, and she needed to stay away from Mitch.

Filling a paper cup with water, she marched out of the room.

Chapter Four

9:00 p.m.—Joanie

J oanie knelt by a poinsettia and slowly poured a small amount of water in the pot. Her heart pounded from her exchange with Mitch, and she fought to steady her shaking hands.

That's right, Joanie, you don't ask; you just do, echoed in her head in the vast stillness of the church. Mitch wasn't right, of course. The decision to divorce him hadn't been made on a whim. She certainly had tried to make him understand how hard it was being married to a man who didn't understand her at all.

She rotated another poinsettia and sat back on her

heels. The plants looked beautiful. So what if Mitch thought she was a quitter? She knew she wasn't.

She touched the soil of another plant, aware that the quiet in the church felt different from the silence of the greenhouse. The very air here seemed more hushed and reverent. She wished some of this feeling would penetrate her heart. It seemed an eternity since she had felt peace.

She bent her head and then heard footsteps. A moment later, Mitch tapped her on the shoulder.

"I didn't mean to upset you. I'm sorry."

Joanie looked up at him. His apology seemed sincere, and she did not want him to realize he still had the power to upset her so deeply. "No big deal."

"It's hard," Mitch added, "talking. I don't know what to say to you anymore."

She knew just what he meant. When they were together, there was this terrible awkwardness as if there wasn't a topic on earth neutral enough to discuss. At the same time, there was something else. Something that, God help her, still felt married to him. Pieces of paper, no matter how official-looking, simply couldn't make her forget what Mitch looked like in his pajamas, the faces he made in the mirror as he shaved, or the way his eyes lit up when he laughed.

Standing, Joanie walked over to the front row and sat in the middle of the pew. After a minute, Mitch slid in beside her.

"Well," Joanie began. "There's always the weather. We could talk about that. That wind is really picking up. Feels damp, too, like there's a storm front moving in."

"That's not what the weatherman says," Mitch replied. "It's supposed to stay above freezing with a sixty percent chance of rain."

All too easily she pictured him in his apartment with the weather channel for his only company. The thought tugged at her heart.

"Well, it feels cold enough to snow."

"Unlikely," Mitch commented.

As they sat in silence, Joanie began to kick her foot up and down. She had the nearly irresistible urge to ask Mitch more personal questions. The girls barely talked about his apartment, and she was dying to know more about it.

"So, are you spending Christmas Day alone?" Joanie's foot swung a little faster.

"No," Mitch replied. "Candy has invited me over."

Candy? Who the heck was Candy? His girlfriend? Unable to stop herself, Joanie said, "Candy is . . . ?"

"A friend," Mitch replied. "She plays the trumpet."

"Yeah, but a name like Candy?"

Jealousy rose like a hissing snake inside her, and Joanie struggled mightily to slay it. They were divorced. Mitch had every right to see whomever he wanted. Just because the thought of dating someone else made her sick inside, it didn't mean that Mitch felt the same way.

"It's short for Candace," Mitch said tightly.

Pride forbade Joanie from asking more. Instead, she sat next to him, swinging her foot and trying to ignore the thought of Mitch dating someone named Candy.

Next to her, Mitch seemed content in the silence. Each even pull of his breath, however, reminded her of his snoring at night. He could, and had, slept through just about anything—kids crying, thunderstorms, even Joanie poking him in the ribs to get him to turn over so he wouldn't snore so loudly.

She wouldn't admit it to him, but when he'd started sleeping in his study, she'd missed the sound of his breath sawing through the night. When she awoke, and this happened pretty much every night, the silence in the room actually buzzed in her ears.

"Candy and I are volunteering together in the music ministry," Mitch continued. "That's what my meeting was about. We're going to work with the youth band."

Joanie had heard enough about Mitch and Candy. She jumped to her feet. "You know," she said, "I just remembered. There's a window in the ladies' room that just might open." Even before Mitch could respond, she moved toward the staircase that led to the basement. "If we can reach it, we might be able to get it open."

"That's a great idea." Mitch's voice rang with enthusiasm. "Let's take a look."

Striding up the aisle, Joanie tried to put some distance between herself and Mitch. Now it was clear why Mitch was so mad about getting locked in the church and eager for them to work together. He couldn't wait to get out of the church so he could go see *Candy*.

"Is that a new perfume?" Mitch asked, following closely as she started down the basement steps. "You smell good."

Joanie made a sound of disgust. How could he be complimenting her perfume when he'd practically announced he had a girlfriend?

And now that she was thinking about it, since when did he have time to lead the church band? Certainly when they'd been married, he'd never had free time. Weekends, he'd been especially busy, using Sunday to catch up on his paperwork. Of course that was all before Candy.

In the ladies' room, she resisted the urge to confront Mitch about his new priorities and instead pointed to a set of high, narrow windows. "See that crank set? Doesn't it look like it'll open that window?"

"Yeah," Mitch agreed. "Those windows are designed to open."

"*If* we can reach them," Joanie said. "It's too high to reach standing and too far from the sink to use the countertop."

"All we need is something to stand on," Mitchell stated. "Where does Pastor Frank keep those folding chairs?"

"In the banquet room closet."

Joanie led Mitchell to the double doors of the oversized cabinet where she and the other members of the Suddenly Single group stored the seats after every meeting.

Mitch pulled the doors open, exposing a completely empty cabinet. "Where are the chairs?"

Joanie blinked. This was where they were stored. If they weren't here, it meant that there weren't any chairs. "I don't know." She shifted her weight, trying to figure it out. "Maybe Pastor Frank ordered new ones and they haven't come in yet." When Mitch didn't reply, she added, "He's been doing a lot of updating in the church."

"I'm beginning to think that maybe we are stuck in here." Mitch rubbed his chin. His eyebrows lifted as if something had suddenly occurred to him. "Guess we're going to have to learn to put up with each other."

Something in his expression sent Joanie's heart thumping. Earlier, she'd wished he'd stop looking at her as if she were a flat tire. Now it was even worse. He was studying her with a softness in his eyes that made her uncomfortable. It looked as if he were considering telling her something.

Silently, Joanie turned away. While she still had feelings for Mitch, she couldn't let her guard down. Probably he was debating telling her something about Candy, and she definitely wasn't ready to hear about that.

Back inside the ladies' room, Joanie stared up at the window and wished it would magically open and she had wings to fly through it. She'd soar into the night, high above the trees and houses and far, far from here.

"Joanie?"

"Yeah?"

"I have an idea." He leaned over. "Climb on."

"What?" Joanie studied his bent posture and hoped it wasn't what she thought it was. "Climb on what?"

"On my back." Mitchell gave her an exasperated look. "That way you can reach the window. We did this once before. Remember when we got locked in our basement?"

She remembered it all too well. It'd happened in their old house just after they'd moved into it. It had been romantic then, shut in the old cellar with the dirt floor and the moonlight shining through the dusty ground-level windows.

"Look, Mitch, I'm sure if we just go back to the chapel, eventually someone will come and let us out."

"It could be hours," Mitchell pointed out. "If Pastor Frank has forgotten us, the next person to open the building might not come until tomorrow night."

She'd be alone with Mitchell for an entire day? Once the prospect would have delighted her. Now, however, it filled her with inexplicable fear. "Okay."

Mitchell crouched and Joanie climbed onto his shoulders. She steadied herself by planting both hands on Mitchell's head. His hair felt surprisingly silky beneath her fingers. She had forgotten, really, how baby-soft it was. The faint smell of his shampoo reached her nostrils, reminding her how she had once loved to pull his head close to hers and breathe, as if she could inhale not only his scent but also his very essence.

Mitchell straightened suddenly, sending Joanie pitching backward.

"Ouch!" Mitchell growled. "Ease up on my hair!"

"I would," Joanie gasped, "if you'd stop lurching around like a drunken camel."

"I'm going to be a balding drunken camel if you don't let go."

Joanie loosened her death grip on his hair. She was prepared, however, to yank it out by the roots if he dared make one comment about her weight.

"Just get the window," Mitchell ordered. "Can you reach it?"

"Don't know." Joanie gazed at the long, narrow pane. She'd have to let go of Mitchell's hair to open it, and she wasn't too sure she could keep her balance without it. "Hold my legs tighter."

Mitchell tightened his grip. "Hurry."

Leaning precariously forward, Joanie strained to reach the top of the window. "I still can't reach it."

"Try kneeling on my shoulders. Like did you did last time."

That was twenty years ago, Joanie thought. How could Mitch possibly think she could still do that?

"Come on," he insisted. "Just do it."

"You're probably hoping I'll fall," she replied, "so you can collect my life insurance."

"You won't fall," Mitchell promised. "Stop talking and get the window open."

"This isn't a very good idea."

Mitchell groaned. "Why do you always have to be so negative?"

"I'm not negative," Joanie snapped. "I'm positive this isn't a very good idea."

"I'll catch you if you fall," Mitchell said. "I promise on my life. However, I have to warn you, my will to live is getting smaller by the minute."

She mentally judged the height of the window and then studied Mitch's shoulders. Shifting her weight, she brought one folded leg to Mitchell's shoulder. "You'll have to brace me."

Mitchell grunted, but grabbed her shin with a hand that felt surprisingly strong. Soon Joanie had the other leg in place and the window jam in reach.

"Hurry," Mitchell urged. "All that dust is tickling my nose."

"I can't turn the crank."

"Try the other direction, for Pete's sake."

Gripping the crank, Joanie pulled backward with all her might. Years of working at a gardening center had given her a strong back and even stronger arms.

Suddenly, she felt something give. At first she thought it was the window jam, but quickly realized Mitchell had lost his grip on her legs. Feeling herself tilt precariously backward, Joanie grabbed for his head and accidentally blinded him.

Mitchell staggered as her weight dragged them both backward. For a moment she thought they might recover, but then Mitchell's feet flew out from under him.

Chapter Five

Amy Williams walked through the garage door and into the kitchen. Dumping her backpack and coat on top of a stack of newspapers, she looked around the kitchen for signs of life. Other than Boris, who looked up sleepily from his basket and thumped his tail, the room was empty.

She flipped on the lights in the family room. In the corner, the artificial Christmas tree stood like an age-weary sentinel who had long fallen asleep on the job. The branches slumped. Decorations that had once dazzled her eyes looked faded and old, particularly those junky paper ornaments she and

33

Natalie had made years ago. She wished her mother would simply throw them away.

Just where was Natalie? Probably volunteering late at the women's shelter. She was such a goody-goody. Sometimes Amy wondered how they could share the same genes and upbringing, and yet be so different. Natalie thought she could save the world, while Amy couldn't even save the salary she earned at her dad's music shop.

Looking away from the mantelpiece where stockings no longer hung from the chimney with care, Amy wished she could turn time back. She wanted to ride around on her mother's hip, or feel her dad's strong arms heaving her into the air. Of course this was a stupid thought. Stupid as looking at that fireplace and wishing there was a fire burning brightly in it. She was fifteen. Old enough to know better than to believe in the magic of Christmas, or in happily-ever-after endings for that matter.

She sank into the couch, frowning. Stacks of brightly wrapped presents slumped around the base of the tree. *So hypocritical*, she thought, *like anyone really cares anymore*.

Standing, Amy wandered into the kitchen. Lifting a container of orange juice, she poured herself a glass. It tasted more bitter than sweet. Wrinkling her nose, she set it on the kitchen table.

She flopped into a kitchen chair and stretched her long legs straight out. Absently, she drummed her fingers along the side of the wooden chair. Her mother had never been a neat freak, but she couldn't remember ever seeing the kitchen this cluttered. Just look at the kitchen table, with its stacks of unopened Christmas cards. Did her mother really think by ignoring the cards she could pretend the holidays weren't happening?

If no one else wanted to, she'd open them. Reaching for a red envelope, her arm accidentally bumped the glass of orange juice. The liquid gushed across the table, fanning out in an orange river and spilling over the side.

Groaning, Amy quickly swept a pile of papers to the side. She grabbed a roll of paper towels and went to work on the mess. By the time she finished, she no longer felt like opening Christmas cards. Instead, she sat in the hard chair and listened to the loud click of the clock.

She held out exactly two minutes and seventeen seconds and then grabbed the telephone. Her fingers trembled as she punched the familiar numbers. Pressing the receiver tightly against her ear, Amy willed the recipient of her call to answer.

On the third ring, she heard the deep, masculine voice answer. She breathed a sigh of relief. "Shane? Thank God you're there."

"Amy." For the first time since she'd arrived home, Amy felt some of the tension easing in her heart. "What's up?"

Tears blurred Amy's vision. For a moment all she could do was hold the receiver and feel emotions clogging her throat. *I'm so alone.* Just thinking those words caused a tiny tear to trickle down her cheek.

She swallowed, ordering herself to say something, anything, and above all to stop crying.

"You okay?" Shane sounded worried.

"Yeah," Amy managed. She fingered one of the three gold hoops on her belly button until she felt steady enough to talk. "Can you come over?"

"Now?"

"Yeah," Amy said, trying to hide how badly she needed him.

"I sort of have this family thing going on." He paused. "It's really lame, but we're all watching *It's a Wonderful Life* for the ten-millionth time."

Clutching the receiver tighter still, Amy fought to shut out the sound of television playing in the background. What she wouldn't give for that to be *her* family.

"I know it's last minute," Thank God her voice sounded almost normal, "but the thing is, I had this really great idea for a new look for our band." She paused. "I was thinking instead of having plain old red hair, we should go black and red. What do you think?"

Shane laughed. "Black and red? Like checkers? That's so rad."

Amy nearly sighed with relief. "Let's do it, then. Tonight. I've got the stuff. You can come over and—"

"How about tomorrow?"

"Please, Shane," Amy pleaded. "No one's home right now, so I wouldn't have to listen to another lecture from my mother about how much better I'd look if I'd only stop dyeing my hair."

"I thought your mom had a rule about us being alone in the house together."

It was Amy's turn to laugh softly. "Mom's at church. She won't be home for hours. Natalie's out saving the world. *Please*, Shane."

There was a long pause and then Shane said, "Hang on a second." The sounds of the TV grew louder, and she heard the murmurs of his parents' voices. She held her breath. What if he said no?

"Okay," Shane said a minute later. "I'll be right over."

Amy grinned in relief. "I'll get everything ready. It's gonna be great, Shane. We'll wear black clothing, too. I've got this great new song about the dark side of the moon . . ."

She heard herself rambling and closed her mouth with effort. Guys didn't like girls who talked their ears off. Guys liked to lead the conversation; otherwise, they just answered in grunts and didn't look at you directly. She knew this from the way her mother and father talked to each other.

"See you in a few minutes, then," Amy said.

"You need me to bring anything?"

"Nah," Amy said. "I'm going to wash my hair before you get here. Just in case I don't get done before you get here, I'll leave the front door unlocked. Just come on inside."

"Okay, babe," Shane said. "I'm on my way."

The words were music to her ears. Amy smiled as she replaced the cordless phone. She knew she'd be grounded if her mother caught her breaking the house rules, but it didn't seem to matter. The emptiness she felt inside hurt more than any punishment her mother could dole out.

And with any kind of luck, her mother would never know Shane had been at the house at all. Amy began to hum a Christmas tune as she jogged upstairs.

Chapter Six

9:30 p.m.—Joanie

With a shrill scream, Joanie toppled to the floor. For a moment she lay there, wondering how she could have been stupid enough to listen to Mitchell and climb onto his shoulders. She was lucky he hadn't broken her neck.

Under her, Mitch groaned. Although this was all his fault, she couldn't help worrying that he might be hurt. "You okay, Mitch?"

"Yeah," he said. "You?"

"Fine." She shifted. "You broke my fall."

She prepared herself for a crack about her weight or the way she slumped over him like a sack of flour. Instead, he just lay there. With his blond hair rumpled and head framed by the tile floor, he gave her a small, sheepish smile.

"I guess this one was higher than our old basement window," he said.

Joanie untangled her legs and sat upright. "We're older, Mitch. Too old to be trying gymnastics."

His eyebrows lifted. "We're not that old, Joanie. We're only in our forties."

Joanie straightened her twisted coat, which had lost several buttons, and tried to regard him with a regal expression. "Don't even think it. I'm *not* trying that again."

"Maybe it wasn't a great idea," Mitch admitted slowly, "but I kind of like how it ended up." His blue eyes stared deeply into her own. "It's a new shampoo, right? That's what I smell."

Joanie scrambled away from him. Here they were, sitting on the cold tile floor of the ladies' room, and Mitch was smelling her hair? The anger seemed to evaporate as well. He was practically transforming before her eyes. The deep line between his eyes had softened. The corners of his mouth lifted into a smile she hadn't seen in ages.

"You'll feel differently tomorrow," she predicted. "When you're sore in places I won't mention. I fell on you, remember?"

He laughed and offered her his hand. "Come on, Joanie, your eyes are smiling. You know you want to give it another try."

"I most certainly do not," Joanie said firmly, getting to her feet without his help. "You must have hit your head when you fell if you think my eyes are smiling."

He ran his fingers through his wavy blond hair in a gesture Joanie recognized well. "What if I sit on *your* shoulders?"

He was teasing, of course. Maybe even flirting? The thought made her heart beat a bit faster. She had to bite her lip to keep from smiling.

Oh, he might seem charming now, but she would do well to remember Mitchell's selective senses. What he didn't want to hear, he didn't. What he didn't want to see, he didn't. He was the Teflon man who used work as an excuse to get out of doing anything he didn't want to do. The old hurt tasted as bitter as a thick lemon rind.

"Let's just go and wait in the chapel," Joanie said at last. "I'm always home by 11:00. When I don't show up this time, the girls will figure out that something happened. The church is the first place they'll look."

"More likely they'll be glad you aren't around to enforce the bedtime curfew."

"Natalie's not like that," Joanie argued. "She'll notice I'm missing."

But would she? The past few meetings Joanie had simply dragged herself home from her meeting. Not wanting the girls to see the tears on her face, she had gone straight to bed.

"Well," Mitch said, "there's always a chance that Candy will stop by my apartment. She knows I was meeting with Pastor Frank tonight. When she finds out I'm not there, she might track me here."

Joanie stiffened at the thought of women casually dropping by Mitch's apartment. Her chin lifted. "Maybe," she heard herself say, "we should keep trying to get out of here."

"You've got an idea?"

Joanie thought hard. "Yeah," she said. "As a matter of fact, I do."

Dusting off her coat, she headed out of the ladies' room.

"Just what are you planning?" Mitch asked as they climbed the stairs.

"We're going to flash the church lights off and on. Maybe someone will see, and realize that we're signaling for help."

"Not a bad idea. But we're pretty far from the street. I doubt anyone could see the church through the pines."

"There's always a chance," Joanie pointed out. "Besides, it's a lot less dangerous doing that than trying to balance on your shoulders."

She searched the wall until she found the light switch. It was a round button, the kind that pushed on or off, or could be turned to dim the lights. She tested the switch, immediately plunging the church into darkness. Another push restored the lights. On, off, on, off. Joanie liked making Mitch appear and disappear at will.

"You don't know Morse code, do you?" Joanie asked, still turning the switch on and off.

Mitch put his hand over hers to stop her dizzying manipulation of the lights. "The universal distress signal is anything sent in a series of three. We'll do three long flashes, three short, and then three longs ones. Like this."

Flashing the lights off and on, Mitch signaled for help.

In each burst of illumination, Joanie glimpsed Mitch's patrician features and intense, deep-set blue eyes. His hair, still more blond than gray, was slightly shaggy-looking in a sexy kind of way.

Were he and Candy serious? If so, then Mitch hadn't spent a very long time getting over her. It hurt to think she'd been replaced so easily. In fact, it made it all the more obvious that he'd never loved her to begin with and validated her decision to divorce him. Knowing this, however, didn't make her feel any better. If anything, she felt a small ache in her heart that threatened to become an even bigger one.

"Here," she said. "I'll take a turn. You can go sit down."

Mitch removed his hand but stayed close. Too close. "Three long, three short."

"Right." Joanie focused her gaze just past Mitch's right shoulder. She would think about her job. Soon the Garden Center would be focusing on spring plants. Trying to distract herself, she recited the names in her mind—marigolds, begonias, impatiens . . .

Flash, flash, flash. Joanie pushed down an image of Mitch staring at Candy with his intense blue eyes. Flash, flash, flash. Were Candy's eyes blue as Texas bluebonnets?

Okay, thinking about spring flowers isn't working, try vegetables, Joanie ordered herself. Flash, flash, flash. *Maybe Candy is shaped like a stalk of celery, or a sweet potato. Yikes, Mitch loves sweet potatoes.*

Was that two short blinks? Joanie had lost track. She added another short blink just to be sure. "So you and Candy are leading the teen band?"

"Yes. We saw the advertisement in the church bulletin and met with Pastor Frank. He wants us to start immediately. He was going to go over the details tonight."

Joanie pushed the light button harder. The darkness hid her look of disgust. Maybe when he married Candy, they'd have kids of their own. Candy was probably ten years younger than herself.

"That's nice," Joanie said. "I'm sure you and Candy will be a smash hit." She flashed the lights faster than ever.

"Thanks," Mitch said. "I know everyone is going to love Candy. She's amazing."

She's amazing. Had Mitch ever spoken like that about her?

Joanie felt a rush of heat sweep through her body. Candy probably shaved her legs twice daily and had never suffered from PMS in her life. Her hair probably was the stick-straight, blond-waterfall type that never tangled, never looked oily, and never needed a touch-up at the hairdresser's.

"Joanie, slow down," Mitch warned. "You're mixing up the long and short signal."

She kept pushing the light switch. She wished it would produce lightning bolts that she could aim at Mitch.

"What's gotten into you?" Mitch sounded genuinely puzzled.

"Nothing," Joanie said. Her fingers, as if they had a mind of their own, continued to punch the switch hard. "I'm signaling for help, remember?"

Mitch laughed.

Joanie scowled. She didn't understand exactly why, but she knew Mitch was making fun of her. If only someone would drive by the church and see their signal. She'd give her right arm to be anywhere but here and with anyone but Mitch.

"What's so funny?"

"You," Mitch explained. "Instead of H-E-L-P, I think you've been flashing out H-E-L-L."

Her hand froze on the light switch, and her gaze found Mitch's. His eyes crinkled in amusement, and a smile wider than she'd seen in years stretched across his face. She used to make him laugh like that, she remembered, before they started fighting all the time.

It seemed ironic that the divorce had restored his sense of humor. And Joanie thought he'd probably laugh even harder if he knew she'd been jealous of Candy.

Chapter Seven

Natalie Williams hurried up the front steps to her house. In contrast, hers was the only home on the street without a single Christmas decoration. She took her key out of her purse, but when she put her hand on the doorknob, it turned easily. What had her mother been thinking to leave it unlocked?

Natalie shook her head, sending great locks of blond hair flying behind her. *Got to talk to Mom about that*, she thought. Dropping a shopping bag to the floor, she heard giggling coming from the kitchen.

She recognized Amy's laugh, deep and infectious. Her father called it a belly laugh, and as always, Natalie couldn't help smiling at the sound of it. She hadn't heard it very often lately, either.

Passing through the family room, she paused to stare at the artificial Christmas tree. Okay, it looked pretty lame, but if she hadn't dragged it out from the attic and decorated it, no one else would have.

Shrugging off her coat, she walked into the kitchen and froze. An undeniably male body wearing what appeared to be her mother's bathrobe bent over the sink while her sister squirted his head with the sink hose. Her sister, also clothed in her bathrobe, glanced up, saw her, and froze.

"Natalie?" she said. "I thought you were volunteering at the women's shelter."

Natalie set her purse on the kitchen table. "What are you doing, Amy?"

"What do you think I'm doing?" Amy pointed to the figure bent over in the sink. "I'm dyeing Shane's hair. And mine."

"Hello, Nat," Shane's voice was garbled from the flow of water pouring over his head.

"Is Mom here?" Natalie looked around.

"Nope," Amy replied. The way she quickly averted her gaze told Natalie that she knew she was going to get in trouble.

"You know the rules. No boys allowed in the house when no one else is home."

Turning, Amy resumed her task of washing

Shane's hair. "You're not my mother," she said. "So butt out."

"Hey, take it easy," Shane said. "You don't want to drown me, do you?"

Amy pushed his head even lower beneath the water. "I have to get this all out."

Looking at Shane's hairy legs sticking out from beneath the bathrobe, Natalie tried not to imagine what else he wasn't wearing.

"If all you're doing is dyeing his hair, how come he doesn't have any clothes on?"

"Well, duh," Amy replied. "If you get hair dye on clothes, it never comes off."

"You're not dyeing his legs, are you?"

Natalie shook her head. Her sister had really flipped this time. Always emotional, Amy's impulsiveness had led her into trouble more times than Natalie could count. Although only two years separated them by age, most of the time she felt more like Amy's mother than sister.

Finally convinced that she'd washed the remaining dye from Shane's head, Amy turned the water off. She wrapped Shane's head turban-style in a white towel. "There." She turned to Natalie. "Wait until you see the checkerboard pattern. I've truly outdone myself."

"I think you've totally flipped," Natalie replied. "And I think that Shane ought to leave before Mom gets home."

Amy sighed. "For Pete's sake, Natalie. We're just dyeing our hair." She rolled her eyes. "Why don't you go back to the women's shelter and help someone who actually wants it?"

Natalie stood straighter. Part of her wanted to do just that—walk away and let someone else handle Amy. She had enough on her mind without dealing with another one of Amy's crises.

"The shelter's closed," she said tightly.

"I'll just get my clothes and leave." Shane stepped toward the family room, but Amy's hand on his shoulder stopped him.

"You don't have to go." She smiled up at him. "We're not finished yet. Let's go upstairs to my bedroom."

Natalie met her sister's determined gaze. Without a doubt, Amy knew she would be breaking yet another house rule if she went upstairs with her boyfriend. Well, maybe this time she'd let her get in trouble. And just as quickly she heard herself say, "That's not a very smart idea."

Amy gave her a death look. "That's not a very smart idea," she mimicked. "Gosh, Natalie, do you realize you sound exactly like our father? It must be hard being Mom, Dad, *and* sister."

Despite herself, Natalie drew back. "Amy," she tried again.

"Would you quit it?" Amy hissed. "You're embarrassing the hell out of me."

For a moment the room went very quiet. Natalie stared at her sister, disliking her intensely and loving her so much it hurt. It struck her suddenly that the two of them had become just like their parents, locked on far sides of issues, unable to discuss anything without ending up shouting at each other.

"Have it your way, then," Natalie said.

Before Amy could reply, the doorbell rang. Natalie's gaze flew to her sister, who returned the look with an equally puzzled one. Who would be ringing their doorbell at nearly ten o'clock at night?

"Maybe it's Dad," Natalie suggested. She looked at her sister's face, which had completely drained of color. Amy knew if their father saw Shane and her in bathrobes, Amy would probably be grounded for the rest of her life.

Amy swallowed. "Oh God."

Natalie pointed to the kitchen. "Both of you, get out of sight. I'll handle this."

"Not the stairs, Shane," Amy called, "he can see them from the front door."

Natalie turned toward the front of the house as Shane and Amy scrambled out of sight. Carefully arranging her features into a neutral expression, she planned the polite but firm way she'd get rid of her father. *Nice of you to drop by*, she'd say. *Mom's at church, and, well, me and Amy are just about to go to bed.*

Pulling the front door open, she braced herself

for the stab of joy and pain that came each time her father stood at the front door like a polite stranger.

Her jaw dropped, however, at the elderly figure standing in the spill of light from the porch lanterns.

"Hello, Natalie," Pastor Frank said. "It's nice to see you too."

Behind thick, horn-rimmed glasses, the senior pastor of Faith Community Church looked down at her kindly. Natalie thought, *What in the world are you doing here? And did something happen to my mother?*

"Pastor Frank?" Her throat felt as if someone had tightened it with a wrench.

The pastor smiled. "I'm supposed to be meeting your father tonight. I'm a few minutes late, I'm afraid. I had an emergency meeting at the hospital."

Why would her father agree to meet the reverend here? Natalie frowned. "My dad doesn't live here anymore. I can give you his new address if you'd like."

"No, I'm certain it was here." Pastor Frank smiled. "It's all in my new PocketPC. My secretary downloaded my calendar onto it. Want to see?"

This was sounding even stranger by the minute. Her father had arranged to meet Pastor Frank here? That didn't make sense, unless it was some sort of a family council meeting that her father used to hold about a hundred years ago. If their mother had known about this, why hadn't she told them? *Be-*

cause she forgot. Now that made sense. Half the time her mother walked around in a fog. They'd nearly had their electricity turned off because she'd forgotten to pay the bill.

"I'm sure your dad is on his way." Pastor Frank rubbed his hands together. "If you don't mind, I'll just wait here on the porch for him."

He had no hat and the tips of his ears were red with cold. His wool coat looked thin and old. The air felt damp, as if it might snow any minute. She couldn't very well leave him standing there, could she? What if he caught pneumonia? Natalie glanced over her shoulder.

A quick glance over her shoulder confirmed that Amy and Shane were out of sight. Hoping they'd stay that way, she pulled the door open wider. "Why don't you come in and call my dad? I'm sure he's probably waiting for you somewhere else."

Pastor Frank smiled. "Thank you, Natalie. That's a great idea."

Chapter Eight

10:15 p.m.—Joanie

After admitting defeat about her idea to signal for help with the church lights, Joanie agreed to try Mitch's plan—picking the lock on the front door.

Silently, Joanie watched Mitchell trace his long fingers along the edge of the keyhole. His hands had been the first thing that had attracted her to him.

He'd been moonlighting at the mall as a pianist. For several weeks before Christmas, he'd played on the lower level, near Sears.

She'd been in charge of the holiday floral displays. However, long after she'd taken care of Santa's holly bushes, she'd gone to hear him play. Standing beside the information booth, she'd watched him play Christmas carols on the baby grand piano. Hour after hour, she had watched those long fingers dance across the piano, filling the mall with such a strong, sweet sound that it seemed to go all the way to heaven. He'd had long hair then, she remembered, and that sheepish, beguiling smile that seemed to go straight from his heart into hers.

"You're in my light," Mitchell growled.

"What light?" The happy memory erased, Joanie stepped away from the door. Although she knew he wasn't angry at her, his tone implied she'd done something wrong. This stung.

"That's the problem," Mitchell said. "We need more light."

"My eyes are good. Want me to try?"

"No."

Squinting, Mitchell stuck a key in the lock. Even in the dim light, Joanie could tell it wasn't going to work. From experience, she knew Mitchell wouldn't listen to her. He'd try every key and every sort of angle. When none of them worked, he'd throw them down in frustration. She braced herself for his anger.

She looked back at the altar, where a large wooden cross hung suspended. Its glossy surface gleamed under several spotlights. For a moment, self-pity rose up in her. Here it was, almost Christmas, and she was locked up with the one person who had perfected the art of making her miserable.

The room seemed colder. Joanie pulled her coat more tightly around herself. She'd sit here until the cows came home before she offered to help Mitch again. Grumpy, impatient, belligerent. That's what he was. Good luck, Candy. Thank goodness they weren't married anymore.

Are you so sure? The question slipped quietly through her mind. She shifted uncomfortably.

"Joanie?"

She turned slowly toward Mitchell. Her eyebrows rose in reply. "What? Am I in your light again?"

"Sorry I snapped at you." He shifted his weight. "I wasn't mad at you. I was frustrated at the lock. I can't pick it."

She blinked, truly surprised at the apology and the admission. "It's okay," she said. "You're a musician, not a cat burglar."

He held out his key ring. "Will you try?"

Before she could stop it, a shot of pleasure sped through Joanie. For him to admit she could do something he couldn't was a rare occurrence.

Taking his key ring, Joanie knelt beside the locked door. "Do you remember," she said, "when Natalie was a baby and locked herself in our bedroom?"

"You called me at work," Mitchell said, "when you couldn't get her to unlock the door."

"And I couldn't pick the lock," Joanie added.

"When I came home," Mitchell said, smiling, "I never heard anyone crying so loudly in my life."

"You would have cried too," Joanie said, trying not to smile, "if you had to stand there listening to your child call to you and not be able to get to her."

"If I had to take the door off the hinges, I would have," Mitchell said. "Or climbed onto the roof and gone through the window."

The smile faded from Joanie's face. In those days, he would have done just that. She bit her tongue to keep from pointing that out. She'd never been able to make him understand there were all sorts of ways for kids to lock their parents out. For husbands and wives to lock each other out, too. But what was the use?

They'd had this conversation a hundred times before. It only made him turn away from her, saying that no matter what he did, it wouldn't make her happy, so what was the point? Or worse, he would agree to try harder and then, in less than a day, be giving the same ultimatums to her and the kids.

Shoving the key into the hole, Joanie blinked back tears.

"You think the kids will worry?"

"No. Natalie is volunteering at the women's shelter, and Amy will probably just shut herself in her room and listen to music the way she does every night."

"You need to talk to Amy," Mitchell said, "about her hair. She needs to stop dyeing it all those wild colors."

Instantly defensive, Joanie replied, "What's wrong with it?"

Mitchell didn't look at her. "She has your gorgeous brown color. I wish she would just leave it alone."

Although she tried to pass it off, her cheeks grew warm with the compliment. "Well, she thinks brown is boring. She wants to make a statement about her looks. It's all tied into the rock band thing." She shot Mitchell a glance. "All the Screaming Mimis have dyed their hair red."

"All they need is clown shoes and they'd look like Ronald McDonald's relatives." Mitchell sat back on his heels. "When I was a kid and part of a garage band, my parents would never have allowed me to do anything like that to myself."

"It's just a phase," Joanie found herself saying. "I think the more we make a big deal about it, the more she's going to fight us."

Privately, part of her agreed with Mitch. She hated seeing their beautiful daughter streaking her hair and wearing all that heavy eye makeup. However, she had a feeling her youngest daughter was struggling with a bad case of teenage identity dilemma. When Amy felt confident enough to stop hiding behind all that makeup, she would return to the fresh-faced girl Joanie missed. Until then, any criticism would only drive her further away from them.

"Well, it's getting out of hand," Mitch continued, "all those body piercings, the tattoos, the clothes."

"I know," Joanie said and jiggled the lock a little harder. "She needs a little more time to sort through things. She'll come around."

"What she needs," Mitch argued, "is consistent limitations and clear boundaries. I say we give her a choice: Either she stops putting holes in herself and wearing as much makeup as Tammy Faye Baker, or she's grounded."

Shaking her head, Joanie sat back on her heels. "We tried that, remember? We couldn't control her. All that ended up was that she started lying to us."

"We weren't tough enough," Mitchell stated. "When she didn't meet her curfew, we should have locked her out. She has to know we're serious about what we say."

Joanie blinked. "There's no way I'm ever kicking my daughter out of our house, or even saying that I will. Home is the one place I always want her to feel welcome."

"She certainly feels welcome to come and go as she pleases," Mitchell pointed out. "And to date a boy who has a smaller vocabulary than our basset hound."

"He would talk if you didn't glare at him."

"I don't glare at him," Mitchell countered. "I check his pupils—to see if they're dilated. For drugs."

"He's a good kid." Joanie's voice rose in frustration. "And you're missing the point."

"And that being?"

"She's looking for something. Something she needs that we're not giving her."

"That's crazy," Mitchell replied. "What is it that we haven't given her? She has a great home, parents who love her even if they're divorced, and a God-given gift for music."

Joanie left the last key dangling from the lock. Her hands shook. "Maybe you should ask her, Mitchell. Ask her how she feels about the divorce and for once really listen to what she says."

Before he could reply, she spun and hurried down the center aisle, past the ropes of fragrant pine boughs tied with cheerful red bows, past the rows of white candles lining the windows.

She heard him call after her, "Joanie, come back."

She didn't stop until she had put as much distance between herself and Mitchell as possible. Sliding into a pew, she knelt on the rug and buried her face in her hands.

He blamed her for the girls' problems, saw her softness as weakness, her love a liability. It was as if they stood at opposite poles with the width of the world between them. She wanted to govern with love, he with a steel fist.

They were like birds flocking in a tree with no

branch strong enough to hold more than one bird at a time. They all sat on separate branches, careful to keep their distance. The family life she'd imagined was nothing like the one she had.

She glanced at her watch. 10:30 p.m. Her stomach rumbled in protest. What food did she have in her purse? A quick search uncovered a package of peppermint Life Savers and something red and fuzzy that at one time might have been a cough drop. She selected the Life Saver.

Closing her eyes, Joanie tried to sleep. When she woke up, she wanted the world to be different. She wanted to look in the mirror and see the look of strain erased from her eyes. She wanted to feel as clean and fresh as new snow.

She jumped when a hand landed on her shoulder. Turning, she stared straight into Mitch's navy blue eyes, which gazed down at her intently. "We haven't finished this discussion."

Joanie blinked. Of course they'd finished. All their conversations lately ended the same way—exactly at the place the argument had started. It was why they had decided to divorce. She blinked again. "What?"

"You said Amy wants something from me. Well, what do you think it is?"

Joanie narrowed her eyes. She didn't entirely trust Mitchell's interest and didn't want to say anything he could later use against her. Yet he'd asked for her opinion and seemed genuinely interested. "Your approval," she said at last. "She wants you to approve of her."

"Approve of what?" Mitchell leaned forward. "Of her taste in body jewelry?"

Joanie waved her hand. "I knew you wouldn't agree with me. Let's just not talk. It's easier that way."

"So you think she wants me to approve of her mute boyfriend, multiple body piercings, and the trash she plays in our garage?" He shook his head. "I'll be dead and buried before I approve of that nonsense."

Joanie sighed and studied her hands. It was no longer his garage, but she didn't bother pointing this out. "You're missing the point again."

"You want me to lie to her? Give her false compliments?"

"Of course not." Joanie bit her lip in an automatic, nervous gesture. "She wants your approval so badly she's willing to do anything to make sure she can't get it."

"Huh?"

Joanie wished she hadn't said anything. Now she'd have to slowly take him through her reasoning, which was a waste of time and energy as ultimately he would dismiss her observations.

"Let me get this straight," Mitch said. "Amy wants me to approve of her, so she acts in a way that causes me to strongly disapprove."

Glancing at him, Joanie saw his brow wrinkled in an effort to understand. Against her better judgment, she decided to try and explain.

"She thinks getting your approval is impossible. Therefore, she is giving herself a built-in excuse not to try."

"Oh come on," Mitchell said. "You don't really believe that psychological mumbo jumbo, do you?"

She slid an inch farther away from him. "As a matter of fact, I do."

"So you think it's my fault that she's so messed up?"

Joanie rolled her eyes. Of course it wasn't. "Absolutely," she said. "I happen to be a perfect parent in every way."

His eyebrows lifted in recognition of the sarcasm in her voice. "Right, and any minute Santa Claus is going to come down the bell tower and let us out of here."

Joanie touched his arm. "Of course it isn't all your fault, Mitch. It's just that," she paused, wondering how he would take it, "even when you lived with us, sometimes it felt like you were somewhere else."

Mitchell's arm stiffened. "I came home every night. It might have been late, I'll give you that. But I was there."

Shaking her head, Joanie wondered how to make him understand. "You might have been there physically, but not mentally."

"You think it's easy owning a music store?" The color in Mitchell's face reddened. "Do you have any idea how fine the margins are? It's not like a nine-to-five job. I *have* to work long hours."

Joanie nodded. The lecture to come was as familiar as the National Anthem. It wouldn't do any good to argue this with him. Usually, when it got to this point, she got up and left the room. Tonight, however, there was no place where Mitchell wouldn't follow her. Not even the ladies' room would be off limits.

"Joanie?"

She kept her gaze on her laced fingers. "Yeah?"

"If I were to try to make Amy feel like she has my approval, how should I do it?"

Huh? Joanie's head swung around. He wasn't lecturing her on how hard he worked at the music store? He actually was considering the truth of her words. Was this some kind of trick?

Mitchell ran his fingers through his dark blond hair. "If you know what to do, just tell me."

Joanie heard the frustration in his voice. "I don't have the answers, Mitch. If I did, we wouldn't be sitting here right now."

They sat in silence. Beside her, Joanie listened to the even pull of Mitchell's breathing. It occurred to her that she could be wrong about Amy, that maybe she was too permissive a parent. Not that she would admit it to Mitchell, but maybe she should stop trying to be Amy's friend as well as parent. It wouldn't kill her to lay down the law a little more clearly.

"Maybe next Saturday, after the music shop closes, I could teach Amy's band a few of the songs I used to play when I was their age," Mitchell said. "What do you think of that?"

"I think it's a great idea." Joanie impulsively reached for his arm and squeezed it.

Mitchell turned to her and their gazes locked. She felt his gaze probing her own, looking more deeply into her eyes than he had done in years. In spite of herself, Joanie felt something in her responding.

"Joanie?" His voice was the texture of suede. Her name was a question on his lips, as if he were surprised to find himself saying it.

Her knee-jerk reaction to keep the distance between them kicked in hard. "It's my turn to try to pick the lock," Joanie said. Her voice sounded strained in her own ears. "Otherwise, a fuzzy cough drop is all we have between us and starvation."

Mitchell lifted his hand and gently pushed the hair off her cheek. Joanie visibly jumped. He looked stricken and confused, as if he could not accept that a touch so soft could hurt her.

"Sorry," he said.

"It's okay."

She rearranged that lock of hair herself. Deciding

to get divorced had been an agonizing decision, but it had been made. Besides, he had someone else now. *Candy.*

"Give me your keys," Joanie stated firmly.

"Well, there's a slight problem," Mitchell told her.

"After you walked off, I tried to pick the lock again." He looked over her left shoulder. "I got a little frustrated and . . . half of it is still inside the lock. It's really jammed now." He met her gaze with an apologetic smile. "Guess we'll have to keep talking to each other." He paused. "Maybe even spend the night together."

Joanie's mouth twisted in horror at the thought. "No way am I spending the night here with you," she declared. "We're getting out of here if I have to climb to the bell tower and scream for help."

Bell tower? Joanie blinked. The old church had stairs that led to the roof. An enclosed tower housed a huge cast-iron bell. Although it hadn't been rung in years, there was a possibility it still worked. If she could ring that bell, it would be sure to attract someone's attention.

There was only one problem—Joanie hated heights. However, the more she thought about it, the more she knew that she had to get out of the church before she did something foolish, like start to believe that Mitch wanted to reconcile.

Before she changed her mind, Joanie marched off to the staircase.

Chapter Nine

10:20 p.m.—Amy

From her hiding spot inside the Christmas tree box, Amy heard her sister say, "The telephone is in the kitchen." A moment later she heard footsteps moving through the foyer.

"What a beautiful tree," an elderly man's voice said.

Yeah, right, Amy thought. Not even all the branches had been installed. She could feel them tickling her feet at the bottom of the box.

"Thank you," Natalie replied.

Wait a minute. The hair rose on the back of her neck. She knew that voice but couldn't quite place it. Peeking her head out, she watched the senior pastor of Faith Community Church follow Natalie into the kitchen.

Amy sank back into the box. *Holy moley. What is he doing here?*

She stuffed her fist into her mouth to keep from laughing. Here she was, crammed into a Christmas tree box that smelled as if Boris had lifted his leg on it. Not only that but she was wearing nothing more than a bathing suit and a bathrobe. The thought of Pastor Frank in the kitchen with her sister while she sat here nearly undid her.

"Would you like a soda? Hot chocolate? A cup of tea?" Natalie asked.

"Tea," the pastor said. "If it's not too much trouble."

"Of course it isn't," Natalie replied.

Water flowed from the tap as Natalie filled the kettle. *Oh no*, Amy thought. Pastor Frank was a talker. She might be stuck in the box until her mother came home. Then what was she going to do? Sashay out as if she hung out in a Christmas tree box all the time?

She wondered what Shane was thinking and, even more importantly, where he was hiding. Her nose itched. It might have been her imagination, but she thought something tickled her leg. It could have been a leftover piece of tinsel, or piece of paper, or a *bug*.

"Here's the phone," Natalie said.

A moment later, she heard, "This is Pastor Frank. I'm at your wife's house, Mitchell. Please give me a call here if you get this message in the next ten minutes or so."

There was a pause and then Pastor Frank said, "Natalie, I'm sorry for the inconvenience."

"Don't worry about it," her sister replied.

The more she thought about it, the more convinced Amy became that something was in the box with her. Any minute she would feel it crawl up her leg. What if there was a mouse nesting at the bottom? She had to get out of the box. But how? The chairs at their kitchen table gave a direct view of the family room.

"Would you like a Christmas cookie, Pastor Frank?"

"Oh no." The pastor said. "My spare tire is getting bigger every day." A long pause and then, "Well, what kind of cookie?"

Store-bought, Amy could have told him. Not the sugary, Christmas-shaped cookies she remembering baking with her mother and sister so many years ago. Nope, the way things were going, he'd be lucky to get a stale Chips Ahoy cookie.

She curled her leg higher and touched something soft and mushy. She jerked her foot away. Ew, gross. She had to get out of this box. Maybe if she wiggled the box slowly, she could move it into the corner and out of sight of the kitchen.

Why hadn't she thought of that earlier? Because she was stupid, she told herself. Natalie had gotten the brains in the family, along with her father's blond hair. However, since her sister had also inherited her father's big nose, she wasn't all that jealous.

"So tell me," the pastor said, "how is everything going?"

There was a long pause. Amy imagined her sister taking a deep breath and trying to put a good spin on the situation. She began to gnaw on her fingernails. Always cheerful, always dependable, that was her sister.

"Great," Natalie began, "we're doing great."

"I don't mean the family," Pastor Frank continued, "I meant you. How are *you* doing?"

There was an even longer pause and then Natalie said, "I'm great," in such a high and falsely cheerful voice that Amy cringed. If her sister were going to lie, she should make it less obvious.

"Divorce is hard on a family," Pastor Frank continued. "It takes time to heal."

Now that was the understatement of the century, Amy thought. It was more like someone had reached inside her and yanked out her guts. It hurt so much all the time that she couldn't believe it. It was sort of crazy, but somehow the jab of a tattoo or body piercing needle helped release some of the inner hurt she carried around inside. She fingered the ring in her belly button and tried to stay still in the box.

Tomorrow she'd get another piercing. Maybe her tongue. She'd always been scared to do it and knew her parents would have a fit. *Yes*, she decided, *definitely my tongue*. Yet even if she did it, she knew getting another piercing would only produce a temporary numbness of her inner pain.

She wasn't like Natalie, who sailed on like a battleship designed to withstand the strongest wind or wave. She didn't seem to need anyone or anything. Sometimes she wished she were just like her, even if it meant having their dad's big nose.

"I know your mom depends on you," Pastor Frank continued. "She's very proud of the work you're doing at the women's shelter."

Amy didn't want to hear more praise of her sister's good works. She inched the box sideways. It made a shuffling sound on the rug, and she froze, hoping no one had noticed.

"I like working at the shelter," Natalie said. "The women who come there have such sad stories. It makes me feel good to help them a little."

"How many hours are you working there?"

"Oh, about twenty," Natalie replied.

"That's very impressive," Pastor Frank said, "to be able to volunteer that much time and be able to keep up with all the work at school."

Yeah, well, Natalie was a genius, everyone knew that. She, Amy, was the screwup. She wiggled a few more inches toward the wall.

"I think I need new glasses," Pastor Frank said in a puzzled voice. "I could swear that box just moved."

Natalie laughed, again sounding so shrill and false that Amy despaired for her sister. "Let me clean your glasses for you, Pastor Frank."

Good. Without his glasses, the old minister was half-blind. She wiggled another inch, and then another. Her nose itched terribly and a huge sneeze filled her head.

"I'm really going to have to get my eyes checked. I could swear that box moved again."

"No, it didn't," Natalie insisted. "Have another cookie."

Amy smiled. Natalie might be irritatingly perfect, but sometimes it helped to have someone so loyal on her side.

"I'm sure it moved," Pastor Frank insisted. "Maybe some animal has gotten inside it."

Amy cringed. What was she going to say if the minister peeked into the box and saw her? She heard the scrape of his chair. Any second she'd hear his footsteps.

"Pastor Frank," Natalie said in a voice that wobbled, "there is something that I need to talk about with you, if you don't mind."

Amy held her breath. Thank goodness Natalie was trying to distract him. If he discovered her, what would she say? *I lost my contact lens in the Christmas Tree box and am looking for it?* Would the pastor know she didn't wear contacts? She didn't even want to think about the penalty of lying to a minister.

But then the chair scraped mercifully against the floor. Amy imagined the senior pastor settling back to listen to whatever Natalie had to tell him. "Go on," he said softly and so kindly that Amy knew if someone talked to her like that she'd tell them anything they wanted to know.

"Well," Natalie said after a long while. "It's about school." Her voice trailed off. Amy had a hard time hearing her. "I . . . well, I'm not going to graduate."

Not going to graduate? Wow, that was funny! Natalie had a straight-A average. Why in the world had her sister picked such a whopper of a lie to tell the pastor?

"I know," Pastor Frank said gently.

What? Amy blinked in surprise. It wasn't a story Natalie made up in order to divert the pastor's attention?

Natalie sighed. "You know I'm failing three subjects?"

"Your mother is quite worried."

Perfect Natalie was failing three subjects? Amy couldn't believe it. For a moment she forgot about the thing in the box with her, the horrific smell, and the way her bathrobe twisted uncomfortably around her body. Instead she concentrated her entire being on listening to what her sister might say next.

Her heart beat faster, and a slow blush of shame spread through her body. What else didn't she know about her sister?

Amy's fingers found the ring in her belly button and twisted it hard. She'd seen Natalie as a measuring stick and herself as always coming up short. She'd been jealous, angry, and—*admit it, Amy*— a horrible sister.

She'd committed the one act that always set her off when someone did it to her—she'd failed to look below the surface. She'd let how someone looked define the person inside.

Inside the box, she settled in and strained to hear what came next.

Chapter Ten

10:15 p.m.—Joanie

The moment Joanie set foot in the dark, narrow stairway, she knew it was a mistake. The stone walls closed around her, seemingly tighter with every step. She'd never been comfortable around heights, and just the thought of stepping out into the open-aired bell tower made it difficult to breathe.

"Joanie, come back." Mitchell's voice came from below. "Nobody is going to hear you scream."

A chill ran down her back. The line sounded like something out of a murder mystery. What if he threw her out of the bell tower and claimed she'd slipped? Her friends would testify that she'd been depressed because of the divorce. Her unfinished

Christmas note would be taped together as evidence. Mitch and Candy would live like kings off her life insurance.

Joanie shook her head. Mitchell wasn't going to murder her. He wasn't a violent person in the slightest. In fact, he had quite a soft heart. He'd cried like a baby when the fish died. Of course, he'd also left her to dispose of the bodies. She squared her shoulders and kept climbing.

"We have to try," Joanie shouted. Her voice echoed off the old stone walls. Just how safe was this staircase anyway? She was afraid to answer her own question. Instead, she imagined the wedge-shaped steps were stone pizza slices. Pizza slices were a lot easier to think about than one-hundred-year-old steps crumbling under her feet.

"Joanie," Mitchell said, sounding closer. "I'm not kidding. You could get hurt up here. Just how old is this tower anyway?"

Starting to breathe heavily, Joanie paused. "You don't have to come up here, Mitch. I'll handle it." She panted a moment, and then couldn't resist adding, "Like I have to handle everything."

The last part of this statement wasn't completely true, but after the way he'd smiled at her in the sanctuary, she felt a self-protective need to put distance between them. She jumped, then, when Mitch's hand landed on her arm.

"You don't have to handle this," Mitch said. "You

stay here. I'll go out in the bell tower and try to ring the bell."

She paused, listened to the thump of her heart, and wondered what to do. If she let him, she'd have to practically embrace him as he squeezed past her. She didn't know if she could handle this. Besides, the steps were so narrow, he might slip and fall. Even if she didn't want to be married to him, she didn't want him hurt, either. She shook her head. "I'm almost there."

She began to climb again, steadying herself against the dark stone walls and feeling sorrier for herself with every step.

Finally, Joanie pushed open a short door and stepped out into the bell tower. She looked over the treetops and twinkling lights of the houses in the distance. Taking a deep breath of fresh, cold air, Joanie fought the rush of vertigo.

Closing her eyes to shut out the unwelcome sensation, she reached out blindly. Her hand connected on something solid and familiar. Mitchell.

Mitchell put his arm around her. "Open your eyes, Joanie, look around you. It's beautiful up here."

Joanie kept her eyes squeezed tightly shut. "Just ring the bell, and then let's get the heck out of here."

"The town is all lit up for the holidays," Mitchell continued. "It's like a private light show, just for us."

Joanie slowly opened one eye. "Stop moving," she ordered. "I think the tower is shaking."

Mitchell's arm tightened around her. "The only thing moving is you. You're trembling."

He was right. She had to get a grip on herself.

"The stars are out, too," Mitchell continued in a soothing voice. "When was the last time we stood outside and looked at them together?"

A long time, Joanie thought, *a lifetime ago.* Before she could stop herself, the image of the two of them, lying on a plaid blanket looking up at the stars, filled her mind. She remembered the fit of their bodies pressed together, the sense of the night sky blanketing them. The stars had seemed so close, and they had been unafraid to wish aloud on them.

She could almost weep for what they had become, two middle-aged people who no longer talked about their hopes and dreams. The stars they saw now in each other's eyes were the ones that came out in anger.

"Lift your eyes and look to the heavens: Who created all these?" Mitchell used his free hand to gesture to the night. "He who brings out the starry host one by one, and calls them each by name." His voice was low and vibrated with reverence.

Mitch spoke the words from the Bible as if they were poetry. And it felt so right to hear him speak the words. She'd always admired this about him, the naturalness of his faith. It just seemed to pour off him, just as the notes of his music had soared off the piano all those years ago. She used to want to be like that herself. But that was long ago, so long ago.

"It is beautiful," Joanie spoke through the lump in her throat, "but freezing. Let's just ring the bell and get out of here."

He shot her a sideways look. She could almost see his mind spinning, wondering if she really meant the words, or if he could ignore them and continue admiring the view.

"Okay." Releasing her, Mitchell stepped forward to examine the bell. "Bet this old thing hasn't been rung in years." He put his hand underneath the bell and felt around for a rope to pull. "It's empty," he reported a moment later. "There's no clanger, nothing inside. Just a bunch of cobwebs."

Joanie frowned. "It's a bell. It's got to make noise. Hit it."

"With what?" Mitchell banged the side of the bell with his hand. The large piece of cast iron didn't make a sound or even budge a bit.

"Hit it harder," Joanie insisted.

"There's no ringer inside," Mitchell said.

"What if I gave you my boot? You could hit the bell with the heel."

Mitch chuckled. "The only thing that would happen would be your bare foot would get cold." He laughed again.

Joanie bristled. This wasn't funny. It was cold,

windy, and scary standing in the bell tower. Worst
of all, Mitchell was right. They couldn't make the
bell ring.

Yet, in spite of all this, Mitch stood there looking
happy, as if all of this were a terrific adventure. He
just didn't get it.

Joanie gazed at the bell. Why couldn't the darn
thing have a ringer? She narrowed her eyes at the
object of her frustration. It just sat there, looking old
and useless. Before she could stop herself, Joanie's
hand formed a fist. Holding her arm like a hammer,
she slammed it down onto the cast-iron bell.

The bell made a small, humming sound, which
Joanie noted in a distant part of her brain. The rest
of her heard only the roar of pain shooting up her
arm. Biting her molars to keep from screaming, she
wondered, dully, if she had broken her hand.

"Joanie." Mitch grabbed her arm. "Are you
okay?"

No. She wasn't okay. It was nearly Christmas and
they were divorced and Mitch had a girlfriend. She
saw all the future holidays lined up in an endless
stream of brightly wrapped packages. She saw herself opening boxes but feeling empty inside. This is
how it would be from now on: Holidays would have
an empty, hollow feeling.

She began to cry then. Her eyes filled with hot,
prickly tears that spilled down her cheek. Her throat
seized as if someone had grabbed her by the throat,

and her hand throbbed painfully to the beat of her heart.

Mitchell's face swam into focus as he bent closer to see her expression more clearly. He stroked the hair off her face and then pulled her against him, murmuring her name and enfolding her in his arms.

Her mouth pressed into the hollow of his neck. She smelled the fragrance of his soap and the night-soaked scent coming off his skin, and sank into these familiar odors.

Mitchell tightened his grip around her. She felt his warmth seeping through her coat, penetrating the layers and years of distance between them. For a moment, she forgot about the divorce, her fear of heights, her frustration at being locked into the church. Even the pain in her hand faded as a flood of wonder shot through her veins.

He didn't try to kiss her, but seemed content to stand there, holding her, holding them together. *If only*, Joanie thought, *he'd done this ages ago, maybe things would be different now.*

But he hadn't, and now it was too late. She shifted slightly in his arms, silently signaling her desire to move away from him. He didn't resist. He never had, Joanie realized. Maybe if he had fought for her, they would have stayed together.

Cold air swirled where warmth had been seconds earlier. Joanie lifted her gaze to Mitch's face. He looked older, somehow. The lines fanning out from his eyes deeper, his skin blotchy from the cold. She saw then that he did get it. He understood that they would not be spending this Christmas, or any other Christmas, together.

"I want you to know something."

She shook her head. "Don't do this, Mitch."

His jaw tightened with determination. "I didn't want this divorce, and now I can see that you didn't either." He stepped even closer to her.

If she let herself look in his eyes, she just might believe him. So Joanie stepped backward until the stone wall pressed against her back. She stared over his shoulder at the lights dotting the night and shivered.

It would be easy, so easy, to step into his arms. And then what? Common sense told her that they'd be at each other's throats before one week ended. It wasn't right for any of them, especially not their daughters, who, God forbid, might end up in the same kind of relationship with their husbands. Besides, what about his girlfriend?

"It's over, Mitch," Joanie said as gently as she could. "I'm sorry."

"Why does it have to be over?" Mitch's voice rang with frustration. "Okay, maybe I wasn't the best husband in the past. I'll admit that I spent too much time at work and not enough with you and the girls. But I can do better." He stepped toward her. "I know what my life is like without you, Joanie. Why won't you give us another chance?"

Because it wouldn't do any good, Joanie thought. *Because of Candy.* "It's the time of year that's making you feel this way," Joanie explained carefully. "The holidays are the hardest times to be alone." She hugged her throbbing hand. "In time you'll see that we're better off apart."

"I don't think so," Mitch stated firmly.

"We want different things," Joanie said as much to herself as to him. "That's why we're always arguing."

Mitch shook his head. "Arguing is part of being married."

"Mitch, I'm not going to argue with you about whether or not arguing is an inevitable part of marriage."

He fell silent then. She heard him scrape his shoe against the wooden floor in frustration. "Arguing," he stated, "isn't what kills a marriage." He stepped away from her until he stood on the far side of the tower. "It's silence that destroys a marriage. It's when two people stop talking to each other."

It wasn't that simple, Joanie thought. He made it sound as if she had simply clammed up for no reason when the truth was they used words like fists. Neither ever won, so Joanie simply stopped trying.

He never seemed to realize that she ached for him to fight *for* her, not *against* her.

She felt the icy drop of a snowflake landing on her cheek. She blinked as other flurries fell in fat, cold blobs around them. The first snow of the winter. Reaching her good hand up, she caught a few in her fingers.

"It's snowing," she said in wonder. "It wasn't supposed to do that."

Mitch laughed as the flurries swirled around them, falling faster and thicker. "Look in the streetlights," he said. "See how big the flakes are?"

Joanie looked at the beams of light. Her throat tightened at the sight of the millions of white dots free-falling in the sky. She hoped they'd stick and transform the earth into a wonderland of white. She wanted a good foot of powder, the kind that squeaked under your boots, blew up against the windows, and lay in drifts against the trees.

"Joanie," Mitch said, "I still love you."

She pretended not to hear him and instead concentrated fiercely on the flakes falling smaller now and harder around them.

"I love you," Mitch said a bit louder.

Maybe they would have a white Christmas this year. Joanie's heart beat faster still. She and the girls would put on their coats and boots and play in the drifts. Have a snowball fight, or build a snowman.

They'd come inside and Mitch would have a great, big fire roaring in the brick fireplace.

Quit it, Joanie ordered herself. *Mitch no longer fit in that fantasy.*

But she couldn't seem to order her gaze away from him. He didn't seem to notice the snow landing in his golden hair, or falling onto the end of his slightly-too-large nose. Instead, he stared right back at her.

"Joanie," Mitch said, "I love you. Do you hear me?"

She heard him, all right, but she'd be darned if she let him know how much those words affected her. Hopefully he couldn't see how her knees shook or how her heart banged in her chest.

"What about Candy?" she said.

"What about her?" he said. "It's you and me. That's the way it's been, and the way it'll always be."

He turned away and leaned over the side of the tower. For one horrible second she thought he intended to throw himself off, but then he cupped his hands to his mouth and began to shout.

"I love you, Joanie!"

Could it be that there, in front of her, looking slightly disheveled but heartbreakingly fierce was Mitch—the old Mitch—the one she'd fallen in love with so many years ago?

Blinking, she stared at him through the curtain of

snow and wondered if she were suddenly breathless from the cold, or if it was the way Mitch was looking at her. Maybe this thing with Candy was not as serious as she thought.

For the first time Joanie began to see that possibly, just possibly, getting locked in the church with Mitchell wasn't such a bad thing after all.

Chapter Eleven

10:20 p.m.—Natalie

Natalie added another heaping teaspoon of sugar to her already-too-sweet tea and stirred. What had possessed her to bring up the topic of her failing grades? Oh, she could tell herself that she'd wanted to divert his attention from the moving Christmas tree box—which surely hid someone inside—but that wasn't entirely the truth. And she knew it.

"Would you like to talk about it?" Pastor Frank asked.

She looked at him sitting there, looking like someone who had all the time in the world. If she had a living grandparent, she would want someone patient like him, someone who would listen to her problems without interrupting or becoming emotional as her mother tended to be.

That was the trouble with parents, Natalie decided. They wanted you to talk to them, but then when you spoke from the heart, they couldn't handle it. Even if they promised not to get upset, they inevitably did. Natalie had learned this the hard way.

Glancing away from the look of concern in his eyes, her gaze traveled to the counter filled with her mother's assortment of potted plants, books, gardening tools, and a pink ceramic pig. She saw, through Pastor Frank's eyes, how out of control the place seemed and felt a tug of shame.

Probably the other houses the pastor visited were clean and beautifully decorated. Other houses probably had the Ten Commandments beautifully embroidered and framed hanging on the walls. Their house not only looked neglected, but it all but screamed of sadness.

"Natalie?" Pastor Frank prompted.

She wanted to talk to him. Just lay everything on the line without censoring it out of loyalty to the family. And yet she feared opening up to him. A lot of stuff was crammed into her head, and she wasn't sure what would happen if she let it all out.

All her life, her parents had told her she was the level-headed one—the one who wouldn't fall apart in a crisis, the one who would look after her sister, the one who was responsible, dependable, and *sen-*

sible. The list went on. Sometimes, like now, she didn't want to be any of those things, and yet it seemed impossible to be anything else.

"I failed chemistry three semesters in a row," Pastor Frank offered. "My parents tried tutoring me themselves, and then they hired someone to tutor me, and then they paid the teacher to tutor me himself."

Natalie lifted her gaze to see if he were really serious.

"They couldn't understand why I wasn't passing," Pastor Frank continued. "Kept asking why a bright young man such as myself couldn't understand a subject enough to make even a C."

Natalie understood. "It had nothing to do with being bright," she said softly.

"It almost killed my father." Pastor Frank sipped his tea. "You see, he had majored in chemistry and then became a doctor. Had quite a thriving family practice. I was the oldest child and the one he saw taking his place when he retired."

"So what happened?" Natalie asked, trying not to appear too interested. "Did you pass the course eventually?"

Pastor Frank set his mug on the table. "The chemistry teacher despaired. Told me that I was the worst student he'd ever seen in his life. The fourth time around he said it'd take a miracle for me to pass and maybe I should give up studying and start praying."

Natalie leaned forward to study the pastor's face. He was smiling now, clearly enjoying the recollection. The wrinkles in his face relaxed, and the expression of peace in his eyes moved Natalie deeply.

"I took his advice," Pastor Frank continued. "I started praying, passed that course, and never took another science course in my life." His fingers, gnarled with age, laced together. "Didn't have to. I knew what I was supposed to do with my life."

"You became a pastor," Natalie finished for him. She stirred her tea and thought about the old reverend's story. "Did you really fail chemistry on purpose?" She couldn't resist asking.

Pastor Frank seemed to take a long time answering. "Maybe not at first, but when I kept falling asleep whenever I tried to study chemistry, I knew the future my parents wanted for me was wrong."

"And your parents," Natalie asked in a voice she fought to make sound casual, "did they get over you not doing what they wanted?"

"My sister took over my dad's practice," Pastor Frank said. "The one who used to faint at the sight of blood." He chuckled softly. "Just goes to show that God has a sense of humor."

Natalie doubted she'd ever look back at this time in her life and laugh. At the same time she knew Pastor Frank had told his story in order to encourage her to follow her dreams.

Natalie sipped her overly sweet tea. As she lifted the mug, her hand shook, sending liquid to slop over the side of the mug.

"What's keeping you from passing?" Pastor Frank asked.

Natalie looked down. She felt as if she'd been carrying around a crushing weight. As the seconds ticked by, she knew that if she wanted to unburden herself, now was the time.

"What do you think of the Peace Corps?"

"Peace Corps? I think it's a pretty good organization."

"I want to join the Peace Corps," Natalie heard herself say. "Go to Africa and teach English to children, or help doctors vaccinate, or dig an irrigation ditch." She looked up, half-expecting him to dismiss her dreams and half-hoping he would so she could let him have it. She'd been researching this dream for ages, and no matter what her parents said, it was more than the idealistic plan of a teenager who had no real life experience.

"The Peace Corps." Pastor Frank stroked his chin thoughtfully. "I can see you doing that."

Momentarily forgetting her sister and her boyfriend, Natalie drew a deep, excited breath. It was such a relief to talk about this to someone who seemed supportive.

"I've been on their web site," she explained, "and *e-mailed* people who are actually doing things like this." She couldn't control the way her hands seemed to move with her words. "What they're doing, it's," she paused and searched for the correct words, "it's incredible, amazing, *important*."

Pastor Frank smiled. "You certainly have the enthusiasm for it."

Nodding, Natalie smiled sheepishly. "My parents had a cow about it," she confessed. "It's the one thing they actually agree on. They think it's too dangerous to go to places like Africa."

"I can understand their concern," Pastor Frank replied, "but sometimes it's more dangerous not to listen to your heart."

"That's what I think," Natalie cried, pleased that finally somebody understood her. "Only," she added, "it isn't going to happen anyway."

"Why?"

She closed her lips firmly. Her family needed her as much as those children in Africa, that's why. How could she leave her mother, who still hadn't gotten over the divorce? Not to mention Amy, who was going to end up looking like a human pincushion if somebody didn't do something soon. That's why she was, and would, make sure she failed courses. If she didn't graduate, she wouldn't have to leave. It was as simple as that.

"I dunno," Natalie hedged, wondering how to tell him the truth without betraying the family. "I guess I'm not as smart as everyone thinks I am."

"Somehow I doubt that," Pastor Frank said. "In fact, I'm willing to bet your SAT scores are pretty high." He studied her expression. "A smart kid like you could probably make up those credits next semester and be on her way to college in the fall. That is, if she wanted to."

Natalie looked away from the compassion in Pastor Frank's eyes. She wanted so badly to tell him that she wanted to do just that. Oh, maybe not to go to college, but definitely go someplace else than here. At the same time, she felt guilty for even thinking about how badly she wanted a fresh start.

"Natalie," Pastor Frank said at last. "If you talk to me, maybe I can help."

She looked up at him. "Everything is fine."

Of course it wasn't. What else was she going to say? Other families probably dealt with divorce so much better than theirs. They didn't fall apart like hers had. She thought about a line from a poem she'd studied in English Lit. *Things fall apart*, T.S. Elliot wrote, *the center cannot hold.*

That was their family to a tee. They were coming apart, more so by the moment. Her mother recognized it but seemed to have no ability to do anything about it. She lifted her gaze to the pastor's face.

"Wouldn't you like another cup of tea, Pastor Frank?"

Without waiting for his response, she jumped up and crossed the floor, her feet sticking with every step. *What was on the floor anyway?* "And another cookie?"

"I really ought to be leaving," Pastor Frank said. "It looks like your father isn't going to meet me here after all."

As she was returning to the table, the telephone rang. Natalie could have cried in relief. It had to be her father returning Pastor Frank's call—or possibly her mother calling to tell her she was on the way home. Natalie snatched the phone off the table.

"Hello," Natalie said.

"Hello," a male voice said.

"Dad, is that you?"

"No, it's Shane," the voice whispered more audibly. "I'm on the back porch, calling from my cell phone. It's freezing out here."

Natalie shot Pastor Frank an agonized glance. "I'm sorry," she said, "but you've reached the wrong number."

She hung up the phone, which immediately started ringing again.

"Hello?"

"I've got icicles in my hair. Is Amy there?"

Natalie chewed her upper lip. She stared at Pastor Frank, who seemed fascinated by the Christmas tree box. A moment later, she understood. The box was moving, slowly, across the floor.

She itched the hives that had broken out on her

neck. "Wrong number." She hung up the phone again.

The box had edged itself nearly out of sight now. Thankfully, the rustling noises had stopped as well. If only Amy would wait just another few minutes. She was sure Pastor Frank would leave.

She dragged her hand through her hair. *I'm the strong one*, she reminded herself, *the one who doesn't panic, the level-headed one, the dependable one . . . the one who's about to freak out here.*

"I may be old and half-blind," Pastor Frank said, "but I know that box moved." He looked from the Christmas tree box back to Natalie. "Just what's inside that box, Natalie?"

She scratched her neck furiously. "My sister, I think."

"Amy?" The pastor laughed. "Very funny. What in the world would your sister be doing inside a Christmas tree box?"

He looked so horrified that Natalie couldn't imagine what he would think if she told him that Shane was on the back porch and dressed in their mother's bathrobe. She covered her mouth to stop from giggling.

After one look at her face, Pastor Frank frowned, glanced over at the box in the family room, and then stood. Walking into the family room, he stood over the old cardboard box. "Amy? Are you in there?"

A muffled voice came from inside the box. "Hello, Pastor Frank."

The giggle worked its way from behind Natalie's mouth. Her tense stomach muscles quivered as the tip of a white towel appeared at the top of the box. A moment later, Amy's face, looking as dignified as a queen's, peered up at her.

"Are you all right?" Pastor Frank extended his arm and helped Amy to her feet. "Goodness, child, what were you doing in there?"

Amy smoothed the sides of her bathrobe. From the glint in her eye and tilt of her sister's chin, Natalie knew her sister was about to deliver a whopper of a lie.

"Before," Natalie started and found herself shaking with silent laughter, "before . . ." She took a deep breath and wondered why something that wasn't funny would make her ache with laughter. ". . . before she answers that," Natalie gasped, "we'd betterresahahahcueShaneahhaha." She heard the sentence melt into a long note of laughter that left her gasping.

"What'd she say?" The pastor's eyes blinked furiously from behind his glasses.

"I don't know," Amy replied, "something about a pain?"

"Sha-ha-ha," Natalie gasped. She clutched her sides as a gale storm of laughter bent her in half.

"Shane?" Amy translated.

"Shane, what?" Pastor Frank asked.

"Back po . . . he . . . he . . . back po . . . po . . . po . . ." Natalie sucked in great gobs of air. Another wave of laughter rolled over her. For the life of her, she couldn't complete the sentence.

"Back porch?" Amy finished.

Natalie nodded vigorously.

"What's going on here?" Pastor Frank asked, his gaze going from one girl to another.

Natalie felt tears roll down her cheeks. Her ribs felt as if they might explode with the force of her pent-up laughter. *There's a simple explanation*, she thought but was unable to get the words out.

And then with Pastor Frank and her sister looking at her as if she'd just sprouted antennas, Natalie, who was always responsible, always reliable, and always in control of her emotions, let it all out.

With Amy demanding, "What's so funny? What's so funny?" Natalie discovered that she couldn't halt the hysterical laughter any more than she could stop breathing.

Just like the poem said, her center couldn't hold together, and Natalie knew she'd finally come apart.

Chapter Twelve

10:30 p.m.—Joanie

Mitchell insisted Joanie follow him down the spiral stairway. That way, he said, if she slipped, she would fall on top of him and his body would block hers from tumbling all the way to the bottom.

Although outwardly Joanie sniffed at the idea, inside she couldn't help the tug of pleasure. Despite their divorce, he still cared enough to protect her from bodily harm. This was more than words, this was an action.

When they reached the main floor, Joanie sighed in relief. She welcomed the open space, not just because of her fear of heights but also because Mitchell's proximity had been equally unsettling.

She could feel herself responding to him with a strength of emotion she hadn't felt in years.

Mitchell reached for her hurt hand. "We probably should put some ice on this."

"It's fine," Joanie insisted. She pulled her hand away. "I was stupid to hit the bell."

His fingers released her slowly, prolonging their contact. "It wasn't a fair fight." He tilted his head to meet her gaze. "There's probably ice in the kitchen. It'll keep it from swelling."

Her hand did hurt, so she let him lead her down the stairs and into the kitchen. In the oversized freezer, Mitchell found a tray of ice cubes. Cracking them open, he wrapped them in a paper towel. Gently placing them on the bridge of her hand, he used his own to hold them in place. "Why is it," he asked, "that you always run off when we're trying to work things out?"

"Why is it that when we're trying to work things out, you always have to win?"

Mitch grinned. "I'm a guy."

"Come on, Mitch. I'm serious. It wouldn't kill you to admit you're wrong once in a while, would it?"

"I don't know," Mitch replied. "It hasn't happened yet." When Joanie tried to pull her arm away, he held on gently. "I'm joking."

"I'm not trying to pick a fight," Joanie explained, "only trying to understand."

"It's human nature," Mitch said slowly, "especially for guys to try to win." He shifted his weight.

"It's the same as not stopping for directions when we get lost." He paused. "Women have their knee-jerk reactions, too."

Joanie held up her hand. "I know. You don't have to give examples."

"The point is that we are different, Joanie. But our differences can make us stronger."

He continued to hold the ice pack in place as she thought about his words. Could it be their separation had changed him? It certainly had changed her.

She looked at the world in a new way. Strangers passed her on the street and her gaze would follow them, wondering if they were as happy as their smiles and sure steps suggested. If they knew something about happiness that she didn't. If she would ever find the key to her own happiness.

Falling asleep at night, she missed hearing Mitch's sleepy voice mumble that he loved her and then become a snore in the next breath.

"It sure is quiet in here," Mitchell commented.

"And cold." Joanie shivered. "Is it my imagination or is it getting colder?"

"It is getting colder," Mitchell agreed.

"Must be the snow," Joanie said, pointing to the stained-glass windows. "It makes the air damper, too."

"It's more than that," Mitch said. "The thermostat must be on a timer."

They sat in silence for a while. "You don't think

something happened to Pastor Frank, do you?" Joanie asked at last.

Mitchell lifted the ice pack and studied Joanie's hand. Satisfied, he replaced the ice. "What do you mean?"

"Well, maybe he slipped on the ice and broke his ankle and had to go to the emergency room, or he had a car accident, or . . ."

Shaking his head, Mitchell chuckled. "Joanie, nothing probably happened to the man. You can't always assume something bad happened."

"But it could have," Joanie insisted. "It's a snowy night, and Pastor Frank *never* misses an appointment."

"I'm sure he's fine," Mitchell assured her. "He's probably sitting at home with a cup of hot chocolate in his hands in front of a roaring fire."

"I don't know," Joanie said. "He lives alone, Mitch. What if he fell in the shower, or had a stroke, or drove his car off the road?"

"More likely he simply forgot about the meeting," Mitch said. "Tomorrow is Christmas Eve, remember?"

"Stress is an immune system weakener," Joanie couldn't resist pointing out. "More people die right around Christmas and Thanksgiving than any other time of the year." When he stared at her, a muscle working in his jaw, she added, "That's a fact, Mitch. I didn't just make that up."

"He's human, and therefore entitled to be forgetful at times," Mitchell said. "Stop worrying."

"Why can't you simply admit that something bad might have happened to him?"

Mitch released her hand. "Because I don't think anything did," he said flatly.

"But it could have," Joanie insisted.

"It didn't."

"You don't *know* that."

Mitch's lips pressed together. She could see him struggling to keep his temper. "You don't *know* that it did."

She tilted her chin to meet his gaze. "For once, can't you agree with me? Can't you say, 'Yes, Joanie, he might have been in an accident, but it's more likely that he hasn't'?"

"I'm trying to ease your mind, for Pete's sake."

"No, you're not," Joanie insisted. "You're putting me down by telling me why what I think is wrong."

"As if I could make you think anything." Mitch snorted. "Once you make up your mind, you'd rather be buried in worms than change it."

He moved a step away from her and crossed his arms on his chest. Joanie's hand began to hurt again, but she wouldn't admit it. Thank heavens she hadn't gone and done something stupid, like blurt out how good his hand had felt on hers.

"Well, I'd rather be buried in worms than be stuck in here with you another moment."

Mitchell's jaw tightened. "Is that so?"

Her chin lifted. "Not only buried in worms," Joanie continued, "but also infested with aphids, mealybugs, and thrips."

"Thrips?" Mitch scowled. "What the hell are thrips?"

"They're insects." Joanie pinched her fingers together to illustrate. "Tiny white bugs that infest a plant and have to be killed by a highly toxic poison."

Mitchell clenched his fists. "You think I'm a thrip?"

"I didn't say that. I said I'd rather be infested with thrips than be with you."

The words came out more harshly than she'd intended. However, she couldn't very well take them back.

"Well, your company is no bed of roses," Mitch declared.

She turned her back to him and crossed her arms. "Let's just not talk."

"There you go," Mitch said, "giving up again just because things got difficult."

"There *you* go," Joanie replied, "trying to win the argument."

"And here we both are," Mitchell pointed out, "arguing over nothing when we could be focusing our energy on something more productive."

He began to walk toward the staircase. His frustration was clear in his clenched fists and the stiff set of his shoulders. "I'm not giving up so easily. We're getting out of this church. Right now."

"That's not soon enough," Joanie added, hard on his heels, and determined to prove she wasn't giving up either.

Chapter Thirteen

10:40 p.m.—Natalie

Clutching her sides, Natalie did her best to stem the hysterical laughter that continued to consume her. Amy needed her to take care of her, and she couldn't do it if she were laughing. Yet one look at her sister, standing there, wearing her flannel bathrobe, made her collapse into a series of rib-aching giggles.

"Natalie, are you okay?" Pastor Frank asked.

She looked at him. Her mouth gaped open and shut like a fish out of water. *Yes, I'm fine*, she struggled to say, and yet nothing other than that awful noise that sounded more like a sob than a chuckle came out.

"Natalie, get a grip," Amy ordered. "This isn't funny."

Of course it isn't funny, Natalie agreed, and almost steadied herself, but then Amy's turban-style towel slipped, revealing strands of black hair wrapped in tinfoil. She looked like she'd stepped off a spaceship from Mars. Natalie lost it again.

"I think she needs a drink of water," Pastor Frank suggested.

"More like she needs us to dump it over her head," Amy remarked. "I've never seen her like this."

Natalie wanted to tell her sister that she'd never seen *her* like this either, but this wildly funny thought only made her ribs ache with the tremendous shaking they were taking.

"I think she's trying to tell us something," Pastor Frank said.

"Probably." Amy rolled her eyes. "That's what she likes to do best."

This comment wasn't so humorous. And after several false attempts, Natalie found if she didn't look at anyone or try to speak, she could stop laughing.

She wiped her eyes on her sleeve. Pastor Frank must have thought he'd stepped into a freak show. There was Amy, looking like some kind of alien; and herself acting like some kind of crazy person who should be hauled off to the looney bin in a straitjacket.

"Shane," Natalie exhaled the word with effort.

"Shane?" Amy repeated.

"Ba . . . ba . . . ba . . ." She sounded like a sheep, and this thought produced a storm of giggles. Get a grip, she ordered herself. "Ba . . . ba . . . ba . . . back porch."

"Shane is on the back porch?" Amy's eyes grew wide. "He must be freezing."

"Let's go," Pastor Frank agreed.

On the back porch they found Shane huddled on the lounger. He'd attempted to wrap the terry bathrobe around himself for warmth. His bent knees stuck up like tent poles.

"Shane!" Amy ran to his side. "Are you okay?"

His lips looked kind of blue to Natalie, who no longer felt like laughing and instead fought the urge to sob.

Her gaze traveled to the screened-in side of the porch. Don't think sad thoughts, she ordered herself, or you're going to start crying the same way you were laughing. Count the stars, Nat, she urged herself. That's always steadied you.

She lifted her gaze to the sky. To her amazement, she saw fat globs of snow falling gracefully. "Hey, everyone," she said, "it's snowing! Let's go outside!"

It seemed so achingly beautiful that she wanted

to run outside without bothering for a hat or coat or even boots. The night sky looked more blue than black, and the trees, dark sentinels that they were, seemed to lift out their branches as if to receive this gift.

"Natalie, have you lost your mind?" Amy pulled her arm. "It's freezing out here. We need to get Shane inside."

The world was a kaleidoscope—why had she not seen this before? Everywhere colors and patterns shifted as she turned. The white concern on Pastor Frank's face, the sparkling silver of Amy's foil on her head, the black spikes of Shane's hair.

If this was what it felt like, she should have let go a long, long time ago. How strange it felt to feel Amy's hand on her arm, leading her inside. Taking care of her. Not once could Natalie recall this happening before.

"Amy, get Shane a blanket," Pastor Frank instructed. "I'll put on the kettle."

As her sister scurried to do just that, Natalie sank onto a kitchen chair. All at once the strength left her body like air deflating from cushion. She wanted to go to sleep.

"Drink this." Pastor Frank pushed a hot cup of tea into her hand and handed another to Shane.

Natalie lifted the hot mug to her lips. The steamy liquid burned her throat, but she sipped it anyway, letting the tea heat the ice inside her. She lifted her gaze to discover Pastor Frank looking at her with concern.

"Better?" he asked.

"A little." Natalie tightened her hands around the mug.

"How about you, Shane?"

"Uh, fine."

"Wiggle your toes around. They'll warm up faster," Pastor Frank ordered. "I can't believe you just stayed there for so long."

Shane didn't reply. He stared down at the kitchen table and then said, "Uh, well, yeah."

She looked up as her sister hurried into the room carrying a pile of fleece blankets. Amy wrapped two around Shane and then, to Natalie's surprise, handed her the other.

"Well, until one of your parents shows up, I think we'll just wait here together." Pastor Frank met the gaze of each person at the table. "In the meantime, does someone want to tell me why Amy was hiding in the Christmas tree box and why Shane was freezing on the back porch?"

Not really, Natalie thought. At the same time she lifted her chin. Amy obviously needed someone to explain everything. She seriously doubted Shane would come to her sister's defense either. She'd never heard him speak more than one sentence at a time.

"It all started . . ." Natalie began at the same time Amy said, "When I came home . . ." and Shane said, "Uh, Pastor Frank . . ."

Pastor Frank held his hand up. "One at a time please." He pointed to Shane. "You begin."

Natalie looked at Shane, who had a blue plaid blanket pulled to his chin. His hair stood straight up in short, black spikes, and light winked from a gold stud in his left eyebrow. Natalie wondered, as she had for the thousandth time, just what her sister saw in him.

"Uh, all I was going to say was that I'd better get going."

"After you explain what you're doing in that," Pastor Frank looked pointedly at the bathrobe, "outfit."

"Getting my hair dyed," Shane admitted.

"I offered to do it for him," Amy blurted out. "I could do yours as well."

"Amy," Natalie said, appalled. "That isn't funny." She pushed the plate of cookies closer to Pastor Frank. "She didn't mean that the way it sounded."

"Of course I meant it," Amy stated. She glared at Natalie. "All I was doing was offering to dye his hair. What's so wrong about that?"

"You were being disrespectful." Natalie dragged her hand through her hair. She pinned her gaze on her sister's face, and then, just loudly enough to be heard, added, "As usual."

"For your information, *Natalie*," Amy said, "I wasn't being *disrespectful*. The pastor at Shane's church actually *shaved* his head, which is a lot more extreme than *hair coloring*."

"Uh, the thing is," Shane said, "Reverend Meyers was pretty bald before."

His comment earned him a glare from Amy. "The point is that I'm tired of Natalie always thinking the worst about me." She fingered the gold hoop on her eyebrow. "She thinks she's my mother." Amy paused and added, "And father."

"Thank goodness I'm not," Natalie shot back before she could stop herself.

"Girls," Pastor Frank said gently. "Arguing with each other isn't going to help. All I'm doing is trying to understand the situation."

Natalie sighed wearily. "It's just like Shane said. He was here getting his hair colored, and then when you showed up . . ."

"Nat, be quiet," Amy ordered. "This has nothing to do with you."

Natalie blinked at her little sister, who for the first time she could remember didn't want her help. A small crack of hurt worked its way from her brain all the way to her heart. Amy was rejecting her help? This wasn't possible. Amy got into trouble; she got her out. This was who they were, and who they had always been. She frowned at her sister.

"When you showed up at the door, Pastor Frank,"

Amy began, "I told Shane to hide and crawled into the Christmas tree box."

"If you were just dyeing your hair," Pastor Frank said gently, "why all the secrecy?"

Amy studied the black polish on her fingernails. "I figured you wouldn't believe we were just dyeing our hair if you saw us in these bathrobes." She shot Shane a glance. "We do have clothes on underneath."

Of course Amy had conveniently left out the part about thinking it was their father at the door. She'd also failed to mention that having a boy in the house when a parent wasn't home was against the rules. The urge to point this out was almost more than Natalie could bear.

"Is that the truth?" Pastor Frank asked Shane.

"Uh, yeah," Shane said. "I found an old pair of her dad's shorts in the closet. Wanna see?"

"No," Pastor Frank said quickly. "But I do feel that everyone here is leaving something out." He looked at Natalie. "I still don't understand why you're failing courses when you clearly want to join the Peace Corps." His gaze turned to Amy. "And I want to know why you're turning yourself into a human pincushion." He took a deep breath. "And most of all I want to know why you dislike each other so much."

"Uh, Pastor Frank?"

"Yes, Shane?"

"I, uh."

"You want to go, don't you? I'm sorry, but you aren't going anywhere until we sort this out."

"Uh, not me." Shane pointed to the basset. "Him. And I think it's too late."

Natalie turned her head to the small pool of liquid by the back door. Boris had had an accident. She rested her head in her hands and wished the floor would open up and swallow her. Quite possibly this would go down in her life history as the worst Christmas she would ever experience.

Chapter Fourteen

10:50 p.m.—Joanie

"Mitch, where are you going?" Joanie nearly tripped over her feet in pursuit of her ex-husband. "What are you doing?"

Mitch had already marched up the steps to the pulpit and was in the process of extracting a purple Advent candle from its candelabra. "Looking for matches."

"Matches?" Joanie hurried up the three steps that led to the altar in time to watch Mitch triumphantly pull out a box of matches. "What are you going to do with those?"

Without replying, he retreated the way he'd

come, determination evident in the set of his shoulders and the fast pace of his steps.

"Would you please tell me what's going on here?" Joanie hurried to keep up with him. "And what are you going to do with the candle and matches?" Was he going to set the whole place on fire?

"I'm getting us out of here." Mitchell kept walking. "That's what you want, right?"

She practically trotted to keep up with him as he descended the stairs to the lower level. "I want out alive," Joanie replied. "Not charbroiled."

He swung the door to the ladies' room open so hard it banged the wall. "Give me a little more credit than that."

She'd give anything to take away that angry edge to his voice and the purposeful way he avoided her gaze. Wide-eyed, Joanie watched Mitchell climb up on the sink. She had to tilt her head to see his head. She swallowed nervously as Mitch struck a match and lit the candle.

"Mitch? This building is really old. If the ceiling catches fire, we're toast."

He raised the candle as if it were an offering. "I'm not setting fire to anything. Look at those smoke detectors. They're state-of-the-art and obviously connected to some sort of monitoring system. I'm going to hold the candle under one of them to make it go off. Someone is bound to hear the alarm and come running."

Rescue? Like a lightbulb turning on, immediately Joanie's attitude changed. They would go home. She would make herself hot chocolate, lock herself in her bedroom, pull the covers up to her chin, and try to forget about this entire evening. Maybe she'd take some Benedryl, which always made her sleepy.

Joanie immediately forgave Mitch for disagreeing with her about what might have happened to poor Pastor Frank. "You're a genius," she declared. "Forget what I said earlier about being charbroiled."

Some of the tightness left Mitchell's face. "Necessity is the mother of invention. I knew we had to get out of here quick before you decided to use my head as a battering ram against the door."

Joanie dismissed the insult with a light punch to his leg. "If this doesn't work, that's a great option." She checked her watch and frowned. "Could you hurry up? I'm a bit worried about leaving the girls alone so long."

Lifting the candle higher, Mitchell held it directly beneath the circular smoke detector. "You'd better cover your ears."

She braced herself as the seconds passed by. "You're sure this is going to work?"

"Trust me," Mitchell said.

The words had barely left his lips when the alarm went off. A high-pitched, ear-deafening shriek filled the room. Mitch looked down in triumph. She watched his lips form the words, "I told you." And then water began to spray from the ceiling.

For a moment, Joanie stood, struck dumb by surprise as the sprinkler system poured cold water over them. *This isn't happening*, she thought. *Any minute I'll wake up and find this was only a bad dream.*

She cupped her hands and felt the cold water pelting down on them. It was sort of like standing on the inside of a fountain, only a lot louder. She'd stood inside a fountain once. It had been—she stomped the thought before it could be completed. She tugged Mitchell's leg. "Let's get out of here," she shouted.

Her wool coat felt heavy as it soaked up the water. Straining through the spray, she glimpsed Mitch fighting to keep the flame alive as he held it almost against the smoke detector. His ears had to be ringing. Hers certainly were.

"Come on." She tugged his leg again.

Before he could reply, the lights went off and they were plunged into total blackness.

Joanie gasped in shock. "Turn the lights back on," she shouted. "Turn them on!"

The room remained pitch black. She couldn't even make out Mitchell's shape, and he'd been standing right next to her a second ago. She blinked and fought the disorientation. Where was the door?

Her ears continued to ring, but gradually Joanie

realized the sound came from inside her head. The smoke detector had stopped screaming. Even the sprinklers had stopped showering them with water.

She reached out blindly and connected with Mitch's leg. "Mitch?"

"Stop pulling my leg," he ordered, "before I fall on top of you."

With effort, she eased her death grip. A moment later, he climbed down from the sink and landed with a thump beside her. She blinked, trying to cut through the layers of darkness and see his face. Adding to her discomfort, cold pellets of water dripped off the end of her hair and rolled down the back of her neck.

"What happened?"

"I think the whole electrical system shorted out." He made a noise of complete disbelief. "We must have blown a fuse somewhere."

Blinking in the darkness, Joanie hoped her eyes would adjust enough to allow her to see the general shapes of things. Was the room growing smaller? She waved her arm around to see.

"Calm down," Mitch said, and caught hold of her hands. "Your eyes will adjust in a moment."

Her heart thumped loudly in her chest. If felt as if someone had drawn a dark hood over her eyes. Even breathing seemed more difficult.

Steady, Joanie, she ordered herself. You've had the lights go out on you plenty of times. Okay, those times she hadn't been soaking wet and locked in a church. She'd always known where the candles were stored, and exactly what to do. Not like this.

A small amount of moonlight filtered through the high, narrow windows. Now that her eyes had adjusted, Joanie could see Mitch's face. His skin glistened with wetness, emphasizing the straight line of his brow bone, the contrasting darkness of his eyes, the familiar set of his mouth.

Joanie wanted to pull back from him. At the same time she wanted to bury herself in his arms.

He brushed the wet hair off her cheek with the tips of his fingers. "You look cute with your hair all wet. Remember our honeymoon in Paris when we jumped into the fountain?" His voice lowered. "You look almost exactly the same."

It'd been the dead of night when they'd done that. They'd stood there, laughing and gasping beneath the curtain of water, and then kissing to seal a pact of love that seemed as eternal as the flow of water over them.

Of course they'd both changed since then. This wasn't Paris, and they had long discovered the flip side of love.

Despite knowing this, her heart began to pound. What if he were to make a new pledge, here under the church's sprinkler system?

His face, so beautiful in semidarkness it hurt, bent toward her. She closed her eyes and tilted her face toward him. It had been so long. So very long since anyone had kissed her, or even held her. The ache inside her seemed to grow bigger with every passing moment.

His hands cupped her face. She could feel herself melting, aching for his lips to touch her own. Why not? Why not kiss him in the moonlight? One last kiss for old time's sake.

Everything seemed to move in slow motion. She could feel herself falling backward in time, until it felt almost as if they were newlyweds, standing in that fountain in Paris.

His breath touched her face, and then the softness of his lips lightly brushed her own. It was a question as much as a kiss.

Lifting herself on her tiptoes, Joanie wound her arms around his neck. She heard the water squish in her boots and Mitch's sigh and then only the sound of her blood roaring through her veins.

"You see, Joanie," Mitch said at last, "it's still there. It's still magic between us."

She blinked at him, struggling to gain control of her emotions. It had been magic between them. It had felt right to be in his arms, but what if it was loneliness that had made it seem so special? And what about Candy? She hadn't forgotten about her either.

"We're also soaking wet." Joanie stepped backward and bumped the counter. "Maybe that's affecting our thinking."

"The water has nothing to do with what just happened," Mitchell said. "Don't be scared, Joanie. This time we can work things out."

"I'm not scared." Joanie shivered. "I'm freezing, that's all."

"I could warm you up," Mitch suggested and stepped toward her.

"Try it and die," Joanie replied.

"What are you so afraid of?"

"Besides being locked in a church with a pyromaniac?" Joanie paused. "That's hard to answer."

"You didn't think I was so crazy when you kissed me. I think you're afraid of yourself, not me." He touched her cheek with the tip of his finger. "Joanie . . ."

"Stop it, Mitch." She jerked away from his touch. "What just happened was a big mistake."

"Not to me," he said. "I'm feeling more alive than I have in months. You've given that to me. Now I want to give you something."

"Unless it's a cell phone, I don't want it." Joanie leaned as far away from him as possible. "You can save the mushy-gushy stuff for Candy."

"There's nothing mushy-gushy about my relationship with her." He paused. "You're not jealous, are you?"

"Of course I'm not jealous," Joanie replied, glad for the darkness which hid the lie that was surely visible on her face. "You're entitled to date whomever you please." *Including a sexy young trumpet player with lungs of steel.*

"Joanie, when you meet Candy, you'll see how off base you are."

She sniffed. "It's really none of my business."

"Hold out your hand," Mitch ordered.

She heard the change rattle as he fumbled in his pocket. "Mitch, this isn't funny."

A moment later he held out a small object for her inspection. "Matches, Joanie, dry matches." In the darkness she heard his lips crack as he grinned. "I knew you'd like those."

He relit the Advent candle, immediately bathing the room in a soft glow. "Better?"

"Much," Joanie agreed, but wasn't sure if it was relief or something else that had made her a bit weak in the knees.

"Come on," Mitch ordered, already turning toward the exit.

"Where are we going?"

"To the kitchen," Mitch replied. "I saw some tablecloths. We can wrap ourselves up in them and get warm. I'll tell you all about Candy."

Chapter Fifteen

11:00 p.m.—Natalie

Natalie cleaned up Boris's mess as the basset watched with sadness-drenched eyes from his basket. "Don't worry," she told the dog. "It was just an accident."

Boris wagged his tail weakly, as if the shame of the whole incident was too much for him. She tossed him a dog cookie and took out the trash. No big deal. She was well used to cleaning up other people's messes.

Shane and Amy had gone upstairs to change. So when Natalie returned to the family room, she found herself alone with Pastor Frank. The elderly clergyman was seated in the chair that her father had favored, an old overstuffed club chair with a matching ottoman.

Just seeing him there, in her father's place, made Natalie's throat tighten up again. Goodness, he'd think she was such a baby if she started to cry. Just to have something to do, she began to bend and separate the artificial limbs of the Christmas tree.

"You love your sister," Pastor Frank stated.

Natalie's head swung around. "Of course."

"So when was the last time you told her?"

An old silver bell dropped off the tree and fell to the carpet. Natalie took her time retrieving it. "She knows," she mumbled.

"Sometimes it needs to be said," Pastor Frank said mildly. "You'd be surprised how many people think they don't need to say those words." He rubbed his hands together. "That reminds me of the couple I counseled a few years ago. They'd been married for twenty-five years, and the woman complained that her husband didn't tell her that he loved her. The man said, 'I told you when we got married that I loved you. If something changes, I'll let you know.' " The old pastor chuckled softly.

"Well, Amy doesn't tell me," Natalie said, stuffing the ornament deep into the branches.

"Tell you what?" Amy said.

Natalie didn't turn at the sound of her sister's voice. Instead she stared at the toilet-paper-roll angel that Amy had made in kindergarten. The wings were actually her handprints cut from white construction paper.

"That you, you know, love me," Natalie said. To her own ears, her voice sounded shaky. "But that's okay," she added quickly. "We don't say that much in our house." She paused. "It's sort of understood."

"Is it?" Pastor Frank asked. "Maybe you two should say it to each other right now."

Natalie turned in time to see her sister roll her heavily mascaraed eyes. Not only had her sister changed out of the bathrobe and into jeans, but she'd also removed the aluminum foil from her hair. Although it wasn't a color Natalie would choose, she had to admit it looked kind of cool.

"You first." Amy grinned at Natalie as if daring her.

What Natalie really wanted to do was wash every bit of makeup, and remove that know-it-all look from her sister's face.

"Okay." Natalie opened her mouth but nothing came out.

"I knew it," Amy declared. "You can't say it."

"Oh please," Natalie said. "Like you don't know how I feel about you. I'm always bailing you out of one problem or another." She lifted her eyebrows. "Take tonight for instance. Who tried to cover for you?"

"Who asked you to?" Amy shot back. "You think it's easy being the sister of Miss Perfect America?"

"Is this female bonding?" Shane asked.

"Quiet," Amy and Natalie said at the same time.

"I'm not Miss Perfect America," Natalie said furiously.

"You act like you are." Amy fingered the gold stud in her eyebrow. "Volunteer work, high school honor roll, always-play-by-the rules." She drew a deep breath. "Even your hair is so perfect it makes me sick."

Natalie involuntarily drew her fingers through her straight blond hair. She'd never thought it was perfect. Never thought anything else about herself was perfect, either. It shocked her to think her sister thought this way.

"I'm not perfect." Lifting her finger to her face, she pointed. "Look at my nose. I've got Dad's honker."

For a moment, Amy looked as if she might laugh but caught herself in time. "It's not that big," she said. "And it fits your face. You've got his eyes, too."

"Well, I don't have his ear for music," Natalie pointed out. "You got all the musical talent in the family. You've heard me in the shower. Boris howls."

"That's true." Amy seemed to brighten and then her expression darkened again. "Well, maybe you're not perfect, but you're awfully close. Sometimes I wish . . ."

"Wish what?" Pastor Frank prodded gently.

"She wishes she weren't my sister," Natalie finished. "She hates me."

"I don't hate you," Amy said. "Well, sometimes I do. But that's just when you get on my nerves, like when I come home from a date and you give me the third degree."

"I do not," Natalie protested.

"You want to know everything." Amy lifted her chin. "Where I went, what I did, who was there, what I talked about. Not even Mom asks all those questions."

Natalie swallowed. The hives on her neck itched terribly. They probably were the size of grapefruits. Although she wasn't supposed to itch them, she couldn't stop herself. Everything Amy had just said was true, but did she really have to say these things in front of Pastor Frank and Shane?

"Can we talk about this alone?"

"Wait a minute," Shane said. "This is just getting interesting."

"Please, Pastor Frank." Natalie drew a hand through her hair, which earned her a hard look from Amy. "I really need to talk to my sister in private."

"Maybe we should take Boris for a walk in the backyard," Pastor Frank suggested. He stood. "Come on, Shane. Let's give these girls a chance to work this out alone."

"Okay," Shane agreed reluctantly. "But Pastor

Frank, I really think we should walk around the neighborhood instead. The little dude," here he pointed to Boris, "leaves land mines in the backyard. It's bad enough during the day, but at night . . ."

"I see your point," Pastor Frank said.

He picked up his coat from the sofa. "We'll be back in about fifteen minutes." He pulled Shane's arm. "This will be a great opportunity for me to talk to you about the youth music program at the church. We need a talented guy like you."

Shane shot Amy a final look as he followed Pastor Frank to the front door. Natalie wanted to chuckle at the silent plea for help in his eyes. Pastor Frank could be very persuasive. If she were a betting person, she would wager that by the time they returned, Shane would be playing in the band that very Sunday.

Still smiling, she looked at Amy to share the thought with her, but the expression faded when she saw the tight set of her sister's lips. The sinking feeling intensified as she realized what she needed to explain to her sister.

As soon as the front door slammed shut behind Pastor Frank and Shane, Amy folded her arms across her chest.

"Okay, Nat," Amy said, "spill it."

Chapter Sixteen

11:20 p.m.—Joanie

J oanie followed Mitchell into the chapel. Now that the entire room was dark, she could see more clearly out of the side windows. Snowflakes dotted the black sky in a steady stream. Already she could see it collecting on the ground and the furry limbs of the pine trees.

"Take your coat off," Mitch ordered.

Joanie hugged her arms around herself. "I'm not taking anything off."

"For a woman who wants nothing to do with me, you sure do think a lot about sex," Mitch said.

Just hearing the word made Joanie's face grow hot. "I'm not the one asking you to take something off."

Mitch held up the stack of tablecloths. "Joanie, you're soaking wet. Take your coat off and wrap yourself in these tablecloths."

Joanie gazed at the material doubtfully. "It doesn't look very warm or big."

"It's big enough." He gestured to her coat. "Come on, Joanie. You're shivering."

"You're just as soaked," Joanie pointed out.

"I'm fine."

"You aren't. Your lips are turning blue."

"You're exaggerating."

Joanie looked at his cold, pale face. A lock of his hair fell onto his forehead in a wet clump. Little drops of water dripped from his coat to the floor.

"What if we both get under the tablecloths?" She slipped off her wet coat. "That way we'll both get warm."

Mitchell blinked. "Are you sure?"

Joanie felt his gaze sweep over her body. She'd worn black pants and a bright red turtleneck. Judging from the gleam in his eye, he liked what he saw and hadn't noticed the five—okay, ten—pounds she'd gained since June.

"You're invited purely for the sake of your body heat," Joanie said. "If you're next to me, it'll be warmer."

Although this was true, it wasn't the entire truth. Joanie wanted to sit next to him.

Although the tablecloth wasn't very thick, she

felt warmer with Mitchell pressed against her. The Advent candle glowed softly, bathing them in a small circle of light. It could have been romantic if they were anyone else but themselves. Joanie felt the familiar tug of self-pity and nostalgia.

If only things had been different between them. She'd never loved another man the way she loved Mitchell. Deep in her heart she knew there would be no one else for her.

And Mitch. What would happen to him? She looked at that ragged hairline. He couldn't even remember to get a haircut. It would get even worse as he aged. What if he had to take tons of prescriptions? Unless someone reminded him, he'd forget.

Prior to the divorce, she'd seen him as unbending and strong-willed, someone more than capable of looking after himself. Now she could see that this wasn't the case at all.

"Mitch," she said. "You need to remarry. Even if Candy isn't perfect, you should marry her."

"What?"

She pulled the edges of the tablecloth more tightly around them. "You heard me. You need to remarry. You and Candy have a lot in common."

He looked horrified, as if she'd just informed him that he needed quadruple bypass surgery. "Marry Candy? Joanie, that's the last thing I want. Look, Joanie . . ."

"What did you eat for dinner last night?"

"Hot dogs," Mitch said.

"That's not dinner," Joanie stated. "I rest my case."

"A home-cooked meal is nice," Mitch argued, "but it isn't a reason to get married."

"You don't know the first thing about taking care of yourself," Joanie continued. "You're probably working horrendous hours, your cholesterol is probably through the roof, and . . ." She pointed at his hair. "You need a haircut."

"Joanie," Mitch said softly, "if I didn't know you better, I'd swear you were worried about me."

She waved her hand as if to make light of his observation. "You're the father of my children," she said. "I'm only pointing this out because *they* need you, in case you didn't know."

"Joanie . . ."

"Boris needs you, too," she continued. "He's not getting as much exercise as he should. I'm sure you and Candy will enjoy taking him for long walks together."

"Joanie, there's nothing between me and Candy but friendship."

She lifted her eyebrows at him. "You don't have to hide the truth, Mitch. I can take it."

"Joanie," Mitch said. "Candy looks almost exactly like your Aunt Thelma. She's not exactly my fantasy woman." He paused. "*You* are."

Joanie imagined her aunt, a plump, gray-haired

woman with lively blue eyes and a fondness for hot pink lipstick. It was easier to think about Aunt Thelma than to let herself dwell on the last part of Mitch's statement. *Me, his fantasy woman?*

"Candy lost her husband about the same time as we divorced," Mitch continued. "We've been helping each other."

"Oh," Joanie said. "I didn't know." She gestured with her hands. "The girls never mentioned her. I just assumed . . ."

"You assumed wrong."

Under the tablecloth Joanie laced her fingers together. She wondered what other things she had assumed about their relationship and been wrong.

"Maybe there's a reason we're locked in this church together," Mitch said quietly. "Maybe we're supposed to stay here and work things out."

She looked at him. "Oh, Mitch, I don't think either of us believes that." She pushed a lock of hair behind her ear. "I know you want us to give it another try. But it's not just us to consider." She paused. "There's the kids."

"What about 'em?"

"They've gone through enough. Natalie used to be a straight-A student. Have you seen her mid-semester report? Three Fs?"

"She told me that those Fs were really incompletes because she was sick and missed her midterms."

Joanie inched closer to him and adjusted the fabric around her shoulders. "Oh, they're Fs all right, and she got them on purpose."

"On purpose?" Mitch repeated. "Why would she do that?"

"So she won't be eligible for early admission at Hamilton Clark College."

Mitchell made a sound of disgust. "She wouldn't do that, would she?"

"Oh yes," Joanie said. "She wants to apply for the Peace Corps instead."

"Is she still talking about that?"

"Yeah," Joanie said. "Didn't you know?"

"No." He stroked his chin the way he always did when something didn't make sense. "If she wants to join the Peace Corps, doesn't she have to graduate high school first?"

Joanie sat up straighter. "I don't know," she said. "I would think she would."

If Mitch were right, why would Natalie purposely be failing three subjects? Why hadn't she thought of asking her daughter this one simple question? She could kick herself for being so stupid.

"So maybe flunking those subjects has nothing to do with the Peace Corps," Mitch said. "Maybe it's something else."

"Like what?" Joanie asked. "She loves volunteering at the women's shelter. She has everything going for her."

"Maybe it's us," Mitch suggested quietly.

Joanie looked at him in shock. "Us?"

Mitch held her gaze steady. "We've put her right smack in the middle of our problems."

Was this true? With a sinking feeling Joanie thought it might be.

For years, she'd been able to count on Natalie to look out for Amy, throw a meal together when she worked late at the nursery, to be her best friend and confidante.

"Maybe we need to talk to her about our situation," Mitch suggested. "Make sure she realizes that she isn't responsible for what's happened."

"And what if the problem is just the Peace Corps? What do we tell her then?"

"Maybe we tell her she can go," Mitch suggested.

Joanie drew back. "Are you crazy? She's just a kid. She can save the world *after* she finishes college."

"Maybe she needs a year to get some life experience *before* she goes to college."

Looking into Mitch's eyes, Joanie felt her muscles tense. "You *want* our daughter to go to Africa?" Before he could reply, she continued. "Do you know how dangerous it is over there? She could get malaria, or dysentery, or AIDS." She paused, thinking hard. "Some of the living conditions over there are very primitive." She gestured with her hands, opening the tablecloth and letting cold air seep between them. "For all we know she could get kidnapped by mercenary soldiers, dragged into the jungle, and held at gunpoint for ransom."

Mitch laughed. "Bad things happen everywhere in the world, Joanie. You can live your life in fear, or you can live your life in faith."

She looked away from him, recognizing the truth in his words but unable to stop imagining horrible things happening to her beautiful daughter. "You don't understand, Mitch. This isn't about faith, it's about common sense. You don't lie down on train tracks and expect your faith to save you. You don't send your eighteen-year-old daughter to Africa, either."

"I'm not saying that I want her to go to Africa," Mitch said. "But I don't want her to live in fear, either."

She felt the unspoken implication hanging in the air between them—that her fears ruled her life. Well, it wasn't that simple. Fear and faith were not always black and white. There were gray areas where they mixed and hung in your mind like storm clouds.

"Bad things happen to good people, Mitch. I see it on the news every night."

"Good things happen, too."

Joanie wanted to hit him. Here he went again, driving her crazy with his optimism and leaving her to carry the burden of her worries alone. An idealistic child shouldn't spread her wings for the first time and fly into the African wilderness. She bit her lip hard until she had control of herself.

"We're parents, Mitch," Joanie said after a long while. "It's our job to worry about our kids."

"I agree," Mitch said softly, "but it's also our job not to impose our fears on them." He squeezed her knee as if to take the sting out of his words. "She's going to be eighteen years old soon, and that gives her the right to do what she wants. I think we should support her."

Joanie released her breath in a blast of fury. "Just once would it kill you to see my point and agree with me?"

"I see your point," Mitch replied, "but you can't put Natalie in a protective bubble. It's more likely that she'll get hit by a car crossing our street than get kidnapped by mercenaries in Africa."

"You're making fun of me," Joanie said, pushing the words out of a throat so tight it hurt.

His fingers caressed her leg lightly. "Joanie, don't you see that if you hold on too tightly, you'll lose her anyway?"

She pulled the tablecloth more tightly around herself, trying to shield herself from the truth in Mitch's words. Soon, Natalie's decisions would be out of her control, like everything else in her life. She looked at Mitch, both envying him for his ability to let go and hating him for the same reason.

"Every day I feel her drifting farther and farther

away." She hadn't meant to speak the words aloud and pressed her lips firmly closed.

"I know what that feels like." He looked straight into her eyes. "To feel that distance from someone you love."

The small hairs on the back of her neck would have prickled if they hadn't been so wet. "So what are we going to do with Natalie?"

"I think we should talk to her together," Mitch stated. "But first we need to fix us before we can fix anybody else."

"That's impossible." Joanie looked down at her hands. "Don't you see? We can't even break out of a locked church. Everything we do together ends in disaster."

Mitch snorted. "I can't believe you would give up on us so easily."

"Stop saying that. I didn't give up so easily. It took a long time."

The air she breathed seemed to thicken. He would not let her comment pass without probing. She concentrated on the movement of the air in her lungs and tried to gather the energy required to defend her statement.

"What happened?" His voice was as soft as the candlelight on his face. "Talk to me, Joanie. I'm ready to listen."

Chapter Seventeen

11:32 p.m.—Joanie

Christmas Eve. Natalie is four years old and Amy is two and a half. She, Mitch, and the girls are gathered around the Steinway piano in the family room. A fire cracks and pops in the fireplace and fills the room with the woodsy smell of burning logs. A tall, skinny evergreen stands in the corner, strategically turned to hide the bald patch among the branches. A paper angel that Natalie made in preschool sits atop the highest branch. No thicker than a pinkie finger, the limb bends under the weight of the paper.

Mitch begins an opening instrumental to "The First Noel."

In a red flannel nightgown, Natalie's long blond

hair hangs halfway down her back. She looks like a little angel. Shoulder-height next to her, Amy's short, dark hair spikes up in a style that refuses to be tamed. The way the two sisters hold each other's hands brings tears to Joanie's eyes.

Mitch plays the first notes and the girls begin singing. Their childish voices have a slight lisp, which makes it sound as if they are singing 'Tha fur-tht No-o-ell." She knows next year they won't sound like this, so she tries to memorize this moment. From the tilt of Mitch's head, Joanie can tell Mitch is struggling not to smile. He slows the pace down as they reach the part of the song Joanie's been looking forward to the most. He plays more softly now so the girl's voices really stand out. "Bored is the King of Israel," the girls sing, totally unaware of their mistake in the lyric.

As soon as the song is finished, Joanie engulfs the girls in a hug. Turning on the piano bench, Mitch enters the embrace. Locked together, Joanie feels the strength of their family flowing from one member to the other. Not wanting to let go, not even for a second, she understands the essential truth about life— it is nothing without love.

"What went wrong?"

Joanie heard Mitch voice the question she'd asked herself a thousand times. How could two people who had loved each other so much become so distant and out of touch? Just what day, what moment, what words had sent their relationship spiraling downward?

"I don't know," she said.

Looking at the huge cross at the front of the church, she searched for an answer that would make sense to them both. It would be easy to say they'd grown apart, and this would be true. Mitch buried himself in his music business while her life revolved around her job at the garden shop and the girls.

At night Mitch worked in his office while she read books in their bedroom. Yet, thinking hard, Joanie knew the problem went much deeper than this.

"We had some good times," Mitch said. "A lot of them, don't you think?"

Joanie sighed. "Yeah, but a lot of arguments, too. Like," she lowered her voice to sound more masculine, " '*Joanie, why do you have to buy the most expensive laundry detergent?*' " Her mouth twisted. " '*Why are the kids eating turkey breast for lunch when bologna is so much cheaper?*' "

He held his hand up. "That was a long time ago. We didn't have a lot of money back then."

She shrugged. "Every time you questioned what I bought, you were really questioning my judgment. You didn't trust me to make good decisions." She paused. "You still don't."

"Joanie, I ask questions, but of course I trust you completely."

"When I wanted to paint the kitchen light green, you insisted on dark green."

"And we compromised, remember?"

"It ended up nuclear waste green." She hugged her chest hard.

"Listen, Joanie, you're talking ancient history. We don't argue about turkey breast anymore."

"Of course we don't," Joanie agreed, "because we never talk. You never come to the door when you pick up or drop off the kids. When we talk on the phone, it's yes or no and then good-bye."

"You think that was easy for me, either?" Mitch replied. "I've been trying to give you the space you said you needed. You know what, Joanie? I'm tired of letting you call all the shots."

"And I'm tired of all the *cheap* shots," Joanie snapped. "We can't be together without going for each other's throats."

"We'll never have a boring marriage," Mitch stated. "But I think if we get some more counseling and spend more time together, we can make it work."

He was willing to get more counseling? And spend more time with her? This wasn't normal. They were arguing—by now he should have stormed off. The coldness of the church must be numbing his ability to argue with her if this were the best retort he could come up with.

He gave her the smile—the boyish, crooked grin that went straight to her heart. When he looked at her like that, it was difficult to remember why she had ever divorced him.

"We belong together." Mitchell's fingers laced with hers. "I may be stupid about some things, but that's one thing I know for certain."

Joanie chewed her lower lip. "All we do is argue, or walk around not speaking to each other. What kind of marriage is that?"

"A normal marriage," Mitchell replied. "We've had ups and downs. We can work this out; I know it." He gazed intently into her eyes. "Joanie, I love you."

They'd come this far; why hold anything else back? "But you love your store even more."

"Are you crazy?" Mitch's voice rose in disbelief. "Sure, I've put in a lot of hours, but that's how it is when you're the owner. Look at the economy. Can you blame me for trying to be a good provider?"

As his voice rose with the conviction of his feelings, Joanie sank back in the pew. The tablecloth fell open, but she hardly noticed the cold air. Of course she couldn't blame him. The trouble was she needed more than food on the table. She needed a companion, a life partner, a best friend.

She looked at the altar, bathed in darkness. They'd

been married right there. Pastor Frank had read from Corinthians, "the two shall be as one." She and Mitch weren't even close to being like that. What made it all the worse was they'd been all those things once. "Of course I don't blame you, Mitchell." Even to her ears, her voice sounded defeated.

He reached for her hand. "I love you, Joanie. I always have. Always will." His grip tightened. "Won't you even look at me?"

"I want more than words," Joanie said. "I want actions. To me love is cleaning up the sheets after someone gets sick. It's giving up watching your favorite TV show because your child has a test the next day and needs your help to study. It's driving the kids to soccer practice, or scooping up dead fish out of the tank . . ." Her voice trailed off as she thought back to years of shouldering problems without Mitch's support. It had taken her a long time to learn not to depend on him, but she had. And every step toward self-sufficiency had taken her further away from Mitch.

Joanie couldn't remember the exact day she'd started thinking about divorce. However, once the idea had sprouted, she couldn't pull it from her mind like the weeds she picked from flower beds. How could someone stay married to a person who could not be counted on to be there when the going got tough?

"I may not have eulogized over dead fish, but that

doesn't mean I don't know what love means," Mitch stated. "It's sticking around even when you know you're not wanted. It's being a good provider and trying like hell to understand why nothing you say or do is ever right." He leaned toward Joanie. "You say love is doing the chores. I say it's something else entirely. It's the way I feel when I look at you when you don't know I'm watching.

"It's seeing bits and pieces of you in our daughters. Love is big and bright and hot as the sun. Love is the beauty in our lives, Joanie, not the dead fish.

"And the sad thing is, every time I try to make you understand this, you close your eyes." He touched her cheek. "Just like you're doing now."

Her eyes snapped open. How could he have misunderstood her so entirely? She hadn't meant love was doing chores. She'd wanted to define love as acts of sacrifice. She could see, however, it was pointless to argue with him.

"My eyes are open now, Mitch, but all I see is two people mad at each other for the ten-thousandth time." She dug her nails into her fists. "We're never going to be what the other person needs."

"Maybe you need to be seeing things with more than your eyes," Mitch stated. Standing, he made his way out of the pew.

"Mitch, where are you going?"

"You'll *see*," he stated. Picking up the Advent candelabra, he made his way down the empty aisle.

What was he going to do? Joanie hoped it wasn't something foolish, like climbing back up the circular staircase and sending smoke signals from the bell tower, or trying to turn on the smoke detector again. She didn't like the set of his shoulders. He looked determined enough to achieve his goal at any price. What if he hurt himself?

"Mitch, wait," she shouted. Her voice rang through the vastness of the church. "Come back!"

Mitchell just kept walking and didn't glance back. Watching the flicker of the candles move farther and farther away, Joanie couldn't help the feeling of loss that deepened with every step he took from her. She thought about his words and the time when their love had been exactly as he'd described it—big and beautiful and hot as the sun.

Chapter Eighteen

11:33 p.m.—Natalie

Spill it. How had it happened that she, who had always looked out for her little sister, suddenly became the weakest link in the family?

Natalie brushed her hair off her shoulders. She'd never realized how much harder it was to be at the explaining end of the stick.

"I'm sorry about grilling you about your dates with Shane," Natalie said at last. "I was a little worried and . . ." She broke a cookie in half and then in quarters.

"Stop mauling that cookie," Amy ordered, "and tell me what really was going on."

Natalie focused her gaze on the crumbled cookie.

Just thinking about telling Amy the truth made her cheeks grow hot. Was this how Amy had felt all those times Natalie had bailed her out, and then asked over and over, *Amy, how in the world could you have done that?*

"Shane and I aren't into drinking and drugs," Amy stated. "We don't smoke, either. I know you think I'm a total screwup, but you can back off."

"I know. I know." Natalie lifted her arm weakly. "The truth is, I . . ." she paused. "I . . . ah . . . I . . ."

"What?"

At the pregnancy center, teenaged girls needed her. Natalie held their hands and spent hours listening. She'd looked at these bruised girls, some so lost, others so defiant, and felt their pain. At the same time, she'd been looking for help for herself.

"Are you sure you weren't checking up on me for Mom?"

Natalie shook her head. "No. Nothing like that." She entwined her fingers and felt small and pathetic. "I wanted to know what it was like . . ." Natalie said. She couldn't meet her sister's gaze.

"What *what* was like?"

"Having a boyfriend."

There, she'd said it. Amy would probably laugh and rub her nose in it. She clenched her fingers together, waiting for her little sister to point out every reason why she had never had a date.

"I thought you weren't interested in boys," Amy

said. "I thought you only cared about saving the world."

"I do want to help people," Natalie replied. "But that doesn't mean I want to do it alone."

"This is so funny."

Natalie's head shot up. "It's *not* funny."

"Of course it is." Amy leaned forward to pull Natalie's fingers apart. "I envied you because you didn't need to be with anyone to be happy."

Natalie blinked. "You're kidding."

"Seriously," Amy said. "You're like the Rock of Gibraltar."

"I'm not," Natalie said. "I'm not even a pebble."

"Nat, I can't believe you're saying this." Amy shifted in her chair. "All my life everyone has compared me to you—and believe me, I didn't do so good on that."

"I've wanted to be like you," Natalie admitted, sitting up straighter. "You're so . . ." She searched for the correct word. "Free. You say what you think. You do what you please. And you don't care what anyone thinks of you."

"Nat, it's no fun to be voted most likely to have a mental breakdown."

"Sometimes I think it would be better to be voted that than most likely to succeed Mother Teresa."

Amy laughed. "You're good, Nat, but you're not that good."

Natalie felt herself relax slightly. "Well, I don't

think you're going to have a mental breakdown, either."

"If you really think that," Amy said slowly, "why do you always jump in and help me out?"

"I don't always," Natalie replied, frantically searching her mind for an example of this.

"It's like you don't think I'm capable of handling my own problems." Amy frowned so hard her eyebrows nearly touched. "I can, you know."

"Then why are you constantly piercing parts of your body?" Natalie pointed at the five earrings that climbed the lobe of her sister's ear. "If it weren't for me, you'd look like a human pincushion."

"Maybe I like how I look."

Natalie cocked an eyebrow at her. "And maybe it's your turn to tell the whole truth."

Almost immediately Amy's fingers rose to the gold stud in her eyebrow. "That is the whole truth."

"And . . ."

Amy scowled. "And it's the one thing I can do when everything gets to be too much . . ." An expression of defiance formed in her eyes. "Okay, I do it when I hurt inside. When I feel like everything is out of my control."

The words hung in the air between them. Natalie looked at her sister and felt the love for her sister expanding in her chest. She knew exactly what it felt like to watch her mother and father become nothing more than polite strangers to each other and have absolutely no control over it.

"I know how you feel," she said simply.

"Of course you don't," Amy shot back. "When Mom and Dad got divorced, I not only lost my mother and father, but also I lost you."

Lost her? Natalie drew back. She'd done her best to "be there" for Amy. Shoot, half the time, she did the laundry, made the meals, cleaned the house. Weren't most of the presents under the Christmas tree her doing?

"You haven't lost me," Natalie pointed out. "Who do you think washed those clothes you're wearing? Who drove you to school this morning?"

"That's exactly what I'm talking about. You took over Mom's job." Amy fingered a cubic zirconium on the side of her nose. "You stopped talking to me. Like sisters."

Natalie eyes widened. Here she'd been trying so hard to fill in the gaps the divorce had left in their family, all the while creating an even larger one between herself and Amy.

"Until I was in that Christmas box," Amy continued, "I had no idea you were failing courses at school." She gazed deeply into Natalie's eyes. "Why didn't you tell me?"

"I couldn't," Natalie said.

"I would have taken your side." Amy leaned forward so no more than a foot of space lay between them. "I would have told her to let you join the Peace Corps." She nodded. "Nat, I think that's the most exciting news I've ever heard."

Natalie shook her head. "I couldn't tell you the truth about failing because it has nothing to do with college or the Peace Corps."

"Then what?"

"I was afraid to leave you and Mom alone," Natalie admitted. "The two of you are a lot alike. I figured you'd both fall apart if I wasn't there to make sure you were okay."

She hardly dared look at Amy, who probably would be angry at her for thinking her incapable of independence. And yet as the silence grew between them, she slowly lifted her gaze. To her amazement, her sister wasn't scowling ferociously at her, or even twisting one of her earrings. Instead, her sister was simply looking at her.

"You'd give up what you want for me and Mom?"

"Of course," Natalie replied. How could Amy ever doubt this? She met her sister's gaze. "I want you to come talk to me the next time you feel like getting a tattoo and any other time too." The words her family seemed to have such trouble saying sprang spontaneously to her lips. "I love you, Amy."

It felt so good to say the words. She found herself grinning, happier than she had felt for a long, long time.

Amy placed her hands over Natalie's. "I love you too, Nat. I really do."

Chapter Nineteen

11:45 p.m.—Joanie

Joanie tracked Mitch's movements by the flickering candelabra. He left their aisle and headed toward the front of the church. Clutching the tablecloth tightly around herself, she hurried after him.

What on earth was he doing on the stage where Pastor Frank preached each weekend? Was he about to deliver his own sermon? Her heartbeat accelerated as she followed the movement of the candelabra. It moved deeper into the nave and then became stationary.

He'd reached his destination. She should have guessed that's where he'd go. In the soft light she watched him shift the piano bench backward. He didn't move for several moments, and this, too, was familiar to Joanie.

The first notes glided softly through the darkness. Plain and simple, each note seemed to bravely attack the silent church and fill the empty spaces with such promise of the melody to come that Joanie's heart seemed to swell in her chest.

As the strain to "Silent Night" filled the church, Joanie's throat tightened. How pure and simple the lyrics and yet how profound. It held all the meaning of Christmas.

She studied Mitchell's dark outline bent over the keyboard, moving with the music, making the piano sing with a lifetime of emotion in each note.

Sitting here, Joanie could almost feel the years slipping away, until she was a young woman again, standing beside the rows of poinsettias and falling in love.

Her lips moved with the beloved lyrics to the ancient hymn.

She wanted to hold her breath, as if she could forever hold onto the image of the candles burning faithfully, Mitchell playing his heart out for her, the ceiling black and endless as if it were the night sky itself.

She forgot about her hair, hanging wet and cold around her face, and the soreness of her hand where she had slammed it against the broken bell. Even her desire to break out of the church seemed as if it had happened long ago.

If Mitchell would play all night, she would stand there and listen. Without knowing exactly how, she knew Mitchell felt the same connection between them. This was how it had been between them when they had first met. To feel like this again seemed nothing short of miraculous.

When he finished, he joined her in the pew. "That's what I wanted to give you," he said simply. "I wanted things to be as they were when we first met."

"That was beautiful, Mitch." Joanie lifted her chin to meet his gaze. As he sank into the pew next to her, she studied his face as she had not done in years. Masked behind the straight line of his lips was a vulnerability that softened her heart to him. "Why did you stop playing?"

It came out wrong, as if she were accusing him of another fault. She touched his arm. "I mean, Mitch, you have a God-given talent."

He shifted his weight. "I never stopped playing."

"Of course you did," Joanie said. Again, she heard her words sound harsh with a nervousness that grew by the minute. "How long has it been since you sat down and played?"

"Not long," Mitchell stated.

"For me?" Joanie spoke the words barely above a whisper.

"A while," Mitchell admitted.

"When you played at the mall," Joanie continued,

"I used to bring the girls. Remember? They were barely more than babies."

"I couldn't perform and keep the store open until nine o'clock every night." There was no anger in Mitch's face, but Joanie noticed the lines deepening in his forehead.

"I miss those times," Joanie whispered so softly she wondered if he could even hear her. "Sometimes I wish you'd never opened that store."

Mitchell's eyebrows rose. "That store," he replied, "has let us live a very nice life."

"If it's so nice," Joanie shot back before she could help herself, "then how come we ended up divorced?"

"You tell me." Mitchell crossed his arms on his chest. "You're the one who had the papers served."

Joanie flung her hands out. "That was pretty awful for me, too."

Putting her face into her hands, she blocked him from view. She didn't look up, not even when his hands gently pulled her hands free.

"Joanie," he said. "You asked why I stopped playing. I have a question for you: Why did you stop believing in me?"

Joanie blinked. *Not believing in him*? He was the most talented musician she'd ever met. "What do you mean?"

"Think back. What happened just after I bought the music store?"

Her gaze narrowed. That was ten years ago. Natalie had been seven and Amy had just turned five. They'd been living over on Lancaster Lane with a cat named Gatsby. Natalie was in second grade and Amy had just started kindergarten. For the first time in years, she'd had a few hours to herself. She'd filled them by taking a job at the nursery. She frowned. Surely this wasn't what Mitch meant.

"I went back to work?"

Mitch nodded. "You didn't trust me to provide for you and the girls."

"You're kidding, right?"

"I bought the shop for you, Joanie."

Joanie shook her head. "This doesn't make any sense. I didn't go back to work because of the money." She ran her fingers through her wet hair. "I went back because I've always loved working with plants and flowers."

For a long minute he didn't say anything. He studied her face. "You never said that. In fact, you seemed more stressed out than before you went back to work."

"That's because I was trying to figure out how to work full time and be a good wife and mom."

"I thought it was because you were sorry you'd married a man who could provide so little money for you."

"The kids were at school and you were always working. You never seemed to see how lonely I was." She wondered if they'd end up arguing again but plunged forward anyway. "I thought maybe you could ease up at the shop if you didn't have the pressure of being the sole provider for the family."

Mitch shook his head. "I knew you were unhappy with me but didn't know why. After a while I sort of accepted that I was always going to come up short in your eyes."

Yet he'd loved her anyway. Joanie felt a pang of guilt. She'd begun shutting the door between them; the one to give up on them; the one who initiated the divorce. Oh, he'd certainly had a role in the dissolution of their marriage, but she hadn't been faultless either.

He rubbed the back of his neck. "We really messed things up, didn't we?"

Joanie laced her fingers together so tightly that it hurt. "Yeah."

"Do you realize we just agreed on something?"

Joanie lifted her gaze at the note of irony in his voice. "Yeah." After a moment she added, "I want you to know our divorce wasn't your fault. I said things that I shouldn't have said to you. I'm sorry for that."

"That's the past now," Mitch said quietly. "We need to figure out what happens next between us. What do you want?"

Joanie blinked. She'd been asking herself that same question for months. Mitch's face, half-bathed in candlelight, reflected his feelings for her clearly. He loved her. At the same time, she wondered if maybe they would be better off as friends. That way they could remain close to each other, but not so close that she could get burned again.

"I want . . ." Joanie began and faltered as the wail of a fire engine sounded in the distance.

"You want," Mitch prompted.

She couldn't tear her gaze away from his face. The familiar arch of his eyebrows, the shape of his nose, those lips that had always fit so well against her own.

The siren wailed again, even louder than before. It seemed irrelevant compared to the emotions coursing though Joanie's veins. She thought about earlier, when he'd accused her of living her life in fear instead of faith. She realized now that she'd been trapped somewhere in the middle, as if faith and fear were opposite ends of a high wire.

This is it, she thought. *I've got to decide which direction to take.* Did she want to live in fear, as Mitch had suggested she did, or in faith?

The siren wailed even louder, as if it were right outside the church, and then cut off abruptly. In the sudden silence, Joanie made her decision. She lifted her gaze, ready to share her response, but found Mitch was looking out the window.

Joanie followed the direction of his gaze. A strong light was cutting through the darkness and heading straight toward the church. Other lights followed. Surely they were the beams of flashlights, which meant they were about to be rescued.

Only moments remained before they were discovered. Joanie knew exactly what she had to do.

Chapter Twenty

Midnight—Amy

Amy glanced up as Pastor Frank and Shane walked into the family room. The elderly minister unclipped Boris, who staggered over to his bed and immediately collapsed, panting.

"You girls okay?" Pastor Frank glanced from her to Natalie. His nose was all red from the cold, and he couldn't quite hide the worry in his eyes.

"Better than okay." Natalie winked at her.

"Yeah," Amy agreed. "I was just about to suggest that I give Nat some blue highlights."

Natalie blinked. "You were?" She touched her blond hair. "I mean, I probably could use a makeover." She smiled at her sister. "And I'd be glad to help you organize your closet."

Amy nearly laughed at the thought. Her closet had all the organization of a leaf pile.

"Good, good," Pastor Frank said. "This is all working out exactly as I hoped."

Amy studied the twin spots of color that blazed in the elderly pastor's cheeks. She had the feeling that Pastor Frank meant more than just her conversation with Natalie. She glanced at Natalie, who looked puzzled as well.

"What do you mean, Pastor Frank?" Natalie asked.

Pastor Frank chuckled. "You're such a nice family," he said after a moment. "I just figured you could work things out if you were given a chance."

More suspicious than ever, Amy turned to Shane. "Do you know what he's talking about?"

"Yeah," Shane replied. "He wanted to let you and Nat duke it out, so we went for a walk."

"No, not that." Amy clenched her fists in frustration. "There's something else. I know it." She narrowed her gaze at Natalie. "We've been played."

Natalie nodded. "Pastor Frank, you didn't show up here by mistake looking for my father, did you?"

Pastor Frank smiled happily. "You are a smart girl."

"What have you done to our parents?" Amy cried.

"I haven't done anything," Pastor Frank replied. He checked his watch. "But I guess it's time to see what miracles the Lord has worked."

"What are you talking about?" Natalie demanded.

"I arranged for them to meet at the church to-night," Pastor Frank admitted. "I figured if they spent time alone together, they'd be able to work through their problems."

Amy groaned. "I just hope they're still alive."

Pastor Frank made a tsking sound. "Trust me. I've counseled a lot of couples. They're fine."

"I can't believe you did that," Natalie said. "You just locked them in the church together? Isn't that against the law?"

"It's kidnapping," Amy declared. "I mean, parent-napping."

"Take it easy," Pastor Frank cautioned. "I didn't lock them in the building. I only arranged for them to meet there."

"My mother and father can't even be in the same room for five minutes without arguing," Amy added. "I can't imagine what would happen if they were stuck together for hours."

"Calm down, kids." Pastor Frank motioned with his arms. "Both your parents are reasonable adults. The fact that your mother hasn't gotten home yet is a good sign. They must be working through their problems."

"Working through their problems?" Amy shook her head. "They aren't even talking to each other."

"If they're just staring at each other," Shane added, "I feel sort of bad for your mom. Your dad never blinks."

"We've been relaying messages between them for months," Natalie added.

"If something bad happened," Amy declared.

"It's your fault," Natalie finished.

"I'm sure everything is going to be fine," Pastor Frank said. "The Lord has performed miracles in that old church."

Amy rolled his eyes. She didn't want a lecture about God or Christmas miracles. "Yeah, right," she said. "And reindeer really know how to fly."

Lifting thick gray eyebrows, Pastor Frank regarded her gravely. "We're going to have to work on your faith, young lady."

Amy felt, rather than saw, the look of warning Natalie shot at her. She rolled her eyes sarcastically but swallowed her comments about faith. "The day my parents get back together is the day that I'm joining the youth band at your church."

The old man grinned. "We need a drummer, Amy, and we'll be glad to have you." He winked at Shane.

"Could we please go check and see if my parents are still at the church?" Natalie asked. "The snow hasn't stopped. I'm really worried."

"Of course." Pastor Frank got to his feet. "Let's go."

As Amy stepped into the snowy night, she heard the wail of a fire truck. With a sinking feeling, she knew exactly where it was heading.

Chapter Twenty-one

Midnight—Joanie

One small step closed the distance between them. Hooking her arms around his neck, she raised her gaze to Mitch's and smiled. "I'm crazy," she said. "Crazy to do this, but it's what my heart is telling me to do."

She stood on her tiptoes and wrapped her arms around his neck. *Oh, yes*, she thought, *kiss me*. Just as his lips closed over hers, a beam of light shone through the windows, swept across the church, and with blinding accuracy came to rest directly on them.

"We're busted," Joanie whispered.

"I don't care if the entire town is out there," Mitch replied and kissed her again.

The beam of light moved away from them. Before Joanie had time to appreciate their privacy, she heard noises coming from the front door of the church. A moment later, a voice shouted, "Open up in there!"

"We can't," Mitch shouted back. "It's jammed."

"Open the door or we're going to break it down."

"We can't open it," Mitch repeated. "We're stuck in here."

"Step back then," the voice ordered. "We're going to break the door down."

The old oak door didn't budge under the first blow. Joanie stepped more closely to Mitch and more than half-hoped the door held. There was still so much to discuss with Mitch, so much to work out.

The blows to the door intensified. A panel splintered and then gave on the next blow. A moment later, the door opened and two police officers stormed down the aisle with their guns drawn.

"Nobody move," one of the policemen shouted. "Ed, check the downstairs."

"Don't shoot," Mitch yelled. "We aren't burglars!"

"We were trapped in here!" Joanie shouted as the policeman continued to advance toward them.

"Step apart," the policeman instructed. "And put your hands in the air."

Joanie quickly lifted her arms above her head. They were about to be arrested. She, who had never even gotten a speeding ticket, was now being held at gunpoint.

"This is all a misunderstanding," Mitch explained.

"Are you alone in the building, sir?" the policeman demanded.

"Of course," Mitch replied.

"I need to see your identification. And yours too, ma'am."

As Mitch handed his wallet to the policeman, Joanie tried to remember where she'd left her purse. "Mine's in one of the pews, I think," she offered. Hopefully they wouldn't go through it themselves to look for her wallet. It was a mess. She'd never leave the house again without cleaning it out.

Just then the other policeman rejoined his partner. "The downstairs is secure."

"Of course it is," Mitch said. "It's exactly as I told you. My wife and I were expecting to meet Pastor Frank here, but when we came, he wasn't here. When we tried to leave, the front door was locked."

"We received an emergency signal from the fire alarm, sir," the policeman said. "We're just following standard procedure." He turned to the other officer. "What do you think, Karl? Is he telling the truth?"

The other policeman shrugged. "Could be, but there's damage to the church. There's a broken pane of glass in a window downstairs, the electricity is out, and the downstairs floor is soaked."

"The sprinklers went off when we tried to signal for help," Mitch insisted.

"Have Hawkins' people check out the wiring," the policeman instructed. "Just to make sure there's no electrical fire. I'm going to take these people back to the station and see if their story checks out."

"Look, officer," Mitch tried again. "We were trying to break out of the church, not vandalize it. Couldn't you tell the door was jammed shut by the wind?"

"What wind?" The officer scoffed. "Snow, yes. Wind, no." He shook his head as if he thought they were crazy. "The door was jammed with something *inside* the lock. Not the wind. The firemen suspected vandalism; that's why they called us."

As if on cue, eight firemen wearing full dress uniforms approached them. Joanie couldn't take her eyes off their heavy black boots, helmets, and air packs on their back.

"This is all a terrible mistake," Mitch said. "I'm telling you, we aren't vandals. We'll pay for the broken window and the water damage. All we wanted to do was find a way out of the church."

Yeah, sure, buddy. Joanie could almost read the silent skepticism in the looks the police and firemen exchanged.

"Do we look like criminals?" Mitch asked.

"Do I look like Santa Claus?" one of the police officers responded without humor.

"If your story checks out," the other police officer said as he snapped handcuffs on Mitch, "you'll be free to go."

"We need to call home," Joanie pleaded, "and let our kids know what's happening."

"You can call from the station," the policeman ordered. "The sooner we get there, the sooner we can get this straightened out."

Joanie resigned herself to the inevitable. Jane Blunt had been a pretty good divorce lawyer, but she wondered what the woman would say if she were called to defend Joanie on a breaking and entering charge.

"Mom! Dad!"

That was Natalie's voice. What was Natalie doing in the church? A dog howled, which sounded exactly like the mournful noise Boris made when following a scent. It couldn't be Boris, though, here in the church. Could it?

A moment later, when a plump brown-and-white dog charged down the center aisle, baying happily, Joanie knew she hadn't been imagining anything. Hanging onto Boris's taut leash was Natalie, followed by Amy, Shane, and, thank heavens, Pastor Frank.

Mitch stepped closer to Joanie. "Looks like the rest of our rescue team has arrived."

"Why are you both soaking wet?" Pastor Frank asked. "Are you okay?"

"We're okay." Mitchell looked at Joanie as if to confirm this were true. She nodded slowly, her gaze following the thick beams of light flowing from the firemen's flashlights as they moved about the church.

Pastor Frank looked both of them over from head to toe. Afterward, he took his glasses off, wiped them on his shirt, and studied them again. "What happened?"

Mitch shook his head. "We got locked inside the church."

"There has to be some mistake," Pastor Frank replied. "I arranged for you both to be here tonight, but never imagined you'd get locked inside." He smiled slowly then. "God works in mysterious ways."

"Just please explain it to the police." Mitch inclined his head to the two officers standing nearby and listening with unabashed interest. "We're about to be arrested on vandalism charges."

"Of course. Of course." Pastor Frank turned to one of the officers. "Officer, these people were here at my invitation. They needed some time alone."

"You sure, pastor?" the policeman said. "We had to break down the front door, and there are other damages as well."

"We'll pay for them," Mitch assured him.

"I'll press no charges," Pastor Frank added.

The policeman's partner smiled and unshackled Mitch's wrists. "You must have wanted out of this church pretty badly."

"We thought we did," Mitch said. He winked at Joanie. "But not anymore."

Blushing, Joanie felt the gazes of her daughters resting on her and the weight of their desire to knit the family together again. She wanted that as well. At the same time she knew this new beginning with Mitch was fragile.

"Mitch and I had some good talks tonight," Joanie said. "But if we're going to rebuild a relationship, we're going to need your guidance, Pastor Frank." She looked at her daughters. "All of us."

"Are you serious?" Amy asked. "Are you and Dad getting back together?"

Joanie nodded. "Yeah." She smiled at Pastor Frank. "Please schedule us for some counseling sessions."

Pastor Frank grinned. "You'll have top priority." He turned to Amy and Natalie. "We all have a lot to talk about." He gave each girl a stern look. "I'm sure they'll be telling you all about what happened tonight. Right?"

When Boris barked, as if in agreement, Joanie laughed along with everyone else. "I think he wants to come to counseling, too," she said.

Looking down at the dog, Pastor Frank smiled. "I

haven't helped many bassets, but he's welcome to come to counseling, just as all of you are."

"We'll look forward to it," Mitch promised. "And now I think I'd better take everyone home."

Chapter Twenty-two

12:30 a.m.—Joanie

Spotlights illuminated an inflatable Frosty the Snowman as Mitch pulled into Shane's driveway. "That thing has to be fifteen feet high," Mitch commented.

"Maybe we should explain to your parents why you're so late coming home," Joanie said. Twisting to peer into the backseat, she realized she didn't know the full story herself. "Amy, why did you dye your hair?"

"The tattoo shop was closed," Amy said.

"Well, if you ask me, with that hair and makeup you look like a vampire," Mitch stated. "People are going to think you hang upside down in your closet between concerts."

Joanie elbowed him hard in the ribs. "*Mitch*."

He shot her an apologetic look. "I approve of the beautiful brown hair that God gave you, Amy. And I'm sure I'd approve of Shane's natural hair color as well—whatever that is."

"Brown, Mr. Williams," Shane said. "Same as Amy."

"Dad." Amy gave her father a death look and slammed the car door behind her.

They were almost to the front door when Shane paused and looked deeply into her daughter's eyes. Amy laughed up at him.

In that moment, Joanie's heart leapt up into her throat. Amy might look tough with those pierced body parts and tattoos, but Joanie knew better. Inside that woman's body she was still a child. All Joanie's instincts urged her to protect her baby. Only too well she knew the more you cared for someone, the more power they had to hurt you. At the same time she knew that the alternative was even worse. A guarded heart was a painfully lonely one.

Mitch shot her a sideways glance. "You think they're going to stand there all night?"

"Be patient, Mitch," Joanie stated. "He's probably working up his courage to kiss her. It's got to be tough with all of us watching."

"Kiss her?" Mitch put his hand on the car horn. "You're going to let him *kiss* our daughter?"

"She's fifteen years old, Mitch. I don't think anything life-changing is going to happen with us sitting here."

"Darn right it isn't," Mitch declared. "Why did we ever agree to let her date in the first place?"

"It's practically Christmas, Mitch, lighten up."

"He's a guy, Joanie. I know how fifteen-year-old boys think."

"We're her parents, Mitch. Our presence alone is an embarrassment."

"Okay," Mitch replied, "I won't honk the horn. How about I flash the headlights instead?"

She turned to see if he was serious. As their gazes locked, she saw in the depths of Mitch's blue eyes that behind the determination was concern for Amy. *We want the same thing*, Joanie realized, *what's best for Amy*. But just what was the right answer?

"How about for tonight we let her be. When we agree on the rules for her dating, we'll discuss them with her together."

This solution sounded so reasonable that Joanie wanted to cheer. However, she didn't want to congratulate herself until Mitch agreed with her, which he hadn't.

"At least let me rev the engine a little." He flashed a crooked smile at her. "I know you're right, but I'm her dad. I have to let her know that I'm still looking after her whether she likes it or not."

From the backseat Natalie groaned. "Remind me never to bring a date home."

"And that reminds me, young lady," Mitch said, "that you and I have to talk about your grades."

"But not tonight," Joanie jumped in. She couldn't bear to ruin the evening with an argument with Natalie.

"I'm sorry, Dad," Natalie said. "I thought I could make up those midterms." She sighed. "But I can't."

"I'm sorry, too," Mitch said gruffly. "For being the kind of dad you didn't feel like you could talk to." He twisted in the seat so he could face her. "I don't know exactly what's going on in your life, but I'd like us to talk. Really talk."

Joanie had to swallow hard to get past the lump in her throat. She could see that Mitch wanted terribly for Natalie to trust him enough to open up to him.

"I love you, Nat," Mitch continued, "and I'm going to do a better job of being your dad."

"I love you, too, Dad," Nat whispered.

In the dim light of the car, Joanie could see the love of her father glowing in her daughter's eyes. She was like a thirsty plant eagerly soaking up love like water.

As the car became quiet, Joanie's attention returned to the teens on the front porch. Under the colorful Christmas lights Amy and Shane stood so closely their breath merged into a small, white puff.

"Hit the horn, Mitch," she ordered.

Mitch needed no further encouragement. Both Amy and Shane jumped as he blared the horn. After a brief pause, Shane gave Amy's cheek a quick peck and disappeared inside.

"I'm beginning to like this boy," Mitch stated.

Amy flopped into the backseat. "You didn't have to do that."

"Sorry," Mitch said and sounded anything but.

"You're lucky," Natalie said. "Dad wanted to hit the horn five minutes ago."

"Dad," Amy said. "Do you know how embarrassing that was?"

"Not nearly as embarrassing as having me chaperone all your dates from now on."

"You wouldn't!" Amy shouted.

"Your mother and I are going to have to set some limits," Mitch continued. "And those rules will be enforced."

"Mom," Amy protested.

"It's for your own good," Joanie said.

Amy released her breath in a hiss of frustration. "Okay, but it's going to look pretty lame when I show up at church tomorrow evening dragging along my parents."

"Church?" Joanie felt her jaw drop open. Before tonight, her daughter hadn't seen the inside of a church since before the divorce.

"Yup," Amy informed them smugly. "Pastor Frank and I had a deal. Shane and I will be playing in the youth band."

"You're playing in the church band?" Mitch asked. "You and Shane?"

"Yep," Amy confirmed. "Tomorrow me and Shane are going to jazz up some of those cheesy old Christmas songs."

Joanie exchanged glances with Mitch. She saw his eyes twinkling and knew he was imagining the look of shock on his daughter's face when she discovered that her father would be leading the teen band.

The rest of the ride home passed in silence. Driving down the darkened streets, Joanie watched the decorations pass by and stole glances at Mitch, who held her hand.

As Mitch pulled into the driveway, he let the car idle. It seemed to Joanie that he wanted to preserve the moment as much as she did. Everything she'd ever wanted was right here in the car.

"Want to come inside for a hot chocolate?"

"It's late," Mitchell said. "Are you sure?"

Joanie nodded. "It's the perfect way to end the evening."

"Well, just for a short time," he agreed.

Joanie reached for her purse at her feet. Frowning, she groped the floor. "Girls, is my purse back there?"

"Not that I see," Natalie replied.

Frowning, Joanie struggled to remember carrying her purse to Mitch's car. So much had happened this evening, she couldn't actually remember if she'd retrieved it from the pew or not.

"I left my keys at the church," Joanie said at last. "Can you believe it?"

"Don't worry," Mitchell replied. Turning, he met her gaze. She saw the fire burning deep within his eyes that spoke of a man who would not back down from the challenge of another locked door, or even a marriage that would have to be rebuilt. "If we found a way out of that church, we can certainly break into our own home."

From the backseat Natalie heaved a long sigh. "It's a good thing I have my key." She opened the car door. "Come on, Amy, I think Dad's trying to work his courage up to say goodnight."

As their daughters walked up the front steps, Joanie turned to Mitch. The atmosphere in the car seemed filled with expectation. Mitch returned her gaze but didn't prompt or try to hurry her. It wasn't his way.

Swallowing, Joanie held his gaze, as the words she'd been too afraid to speak all evening hovered at the back of her throat. When was the last time she had spoken them? She wondered why the words were so hard to say, even when she knew they were the right ones to start their new journey together.

Reaching for Mitch's hands, Joanie squeezed them tightly. She felt nervous as a bride and yet just as hopeful. "I love you," she said.

Together, they walked up the stairs and into the house.

Epilogue

Thelma Darber reached into her mailbox and pulled out a thick stack of magazines and envelopes. Now that the holidays had passed, she would have thought all those catalogs would stop coming. Flipping through the pile, she realized she couldn't have been more wrong. Everyone, it seemed, was having a huge January sale.

And then she saw it, a cheerful red envelope tucked between her National Retirement Organization's newsletter and a bill from Fierson's Department Store. Chuckling softly, she wondered who'd been late getting their Christmas cards out.

She didn't have to wonder long. Joanie Williams'

name was right there on the return address. She paused on the porch. She'd wondered why her niece hadn't sent her a card, but had figured with the poor thing's divorce and all, maybe she hadn't sent cards this year at all.

Inside the small ranch-style house, Thelma got herself a hot cup of tea and sank into her padded rocking chair. Smiling, she ripped open the envelope.

Dear Friends and Family, she read.

Happy New Year!

Sorry this card is so late and I hope your holidays were filled with joy and love. I've loved hearing all your news—so thank you for the cards and letters.

I don't have a good excuse for not getting my Christmas cards out on time, unless you count getting locked in a church and then nearly arrested. (please see enclosed news clipping)."

Thelma unfolded the page of newsprint. Above a pretty, white church with a not-so-pretty smashed-in front door, a headline read, "Station 45 Rescues Couple Trapped in Church." *Good heavens*, Thelma thought as she quickly skimmed the article. *What has my niece gotten herself into this time?*

After receiving a code alarm, at approximately 11:45 p.m. Wednesday evening, Station 45 was dis-

patched to Faith Community Church. Upon arrival, they found Hartsdale residents Mitchell and Joanie Williams locked inside the church despite several hours of work to free themselves.

"We tried everything," said Mrs. Williams. "Breaking a window, shouting from the bell tower, and signaling for help with the lights."

According to Pastor Frank Farlow, the couple had come to the church to meet with him. "It was a terrible misunderstanding," said Farlow. "We've never had anyone locked in our church before."

"We set off the fire alarm as a last resort," said Mitchell Williams. "We weren't counting on flooding the building. We plan to pay for all damages, of course."

What makes this story all the more remarkable is that the couple, who have been divorced for six months . . . have decided to reconcile.

Thelma smiled as she skimmed to the end of the article and the fire chief concluded, *"We've rescued many people before, but this is the first time we've helped to rescue a marriage."*

Putting down the article, Thelma returned to her niece's letter. Her smile broadened as she read the rest of their news.

We're all going to counseling, even Boris. Mostly Boris just snoozes, but Mitch and I are doing much better at listening to each other and to our kids. Natalie is going to summer school to make up some credits. Amy is playing in the church band. She and Shane are the only kids there with blue highlights in their hair. Mitch says we have to pick our fights and who really cares what color her hair is. Besides, it makes it easy to find her in a crowd.

I am happy and grateful for the blessings in my life. Not the least of which is learning that it's never too late to start over and the best Christmas gift is simply being with the people you love.

That said, I send all my love and best wishes for a healthy, happy New Year.

—Joanie, Mitch, Natalie, Amy & Boris